"Marry me...and you'll have everything you want, Leigh.

"What your sisters covet...what your father denied you and more."

Her head whirled with Richard's words, all of them striking such painful places.

"I hand you the keys to the whole Durant empire, everything Lawrence acquired in his ruthless drive for power. And no one will scorn you again, or treat you in a contemptible manner. As my wife, you will be my queen, in every sense."

The low throb of his voice was like a drumbeat on her heart.

"Only you can satisfy me. Only you. We're two of a kind, Leigh. You and I...."

Initially a French/English teacher, **Emma Darcy** changed careers to computer programming before marriage and motherhood settled her into a community life. Creative urges were channeled into oil painting, pottery, designing and overseeing the construction and decorating of two homes, all in the midst of keeping up with three lively sons and the very social life of her businessman husband, Frank. Very much a people person, and always interested in relationships, she finds the world of romance fiction a happy one and the challenge of creating her own cast of characters very addictive. She enjoys traveling, and her experiences often find their way into her books. Emma Darcy lives on a country property in New South Wales, Australia.

Books by *Emma Darcy*

HARLEQUIN PRESENTS®

Also available in MIRA® Books
THE SECRETS WITHIN

EMMA DARCY

Bride of His Choice

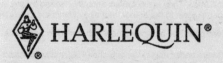

TORONTO • NEW YORK • LONDON
AMSTERDAM • PARIS • SYDNEY • HAMBURG
STOCKHOLM • ATHENS • TOKYO • MILAN • MADRID
PRAGUE • WARSAW • BUDAPEST • AUCKLAND

For Pearl Grant, with much love and appreciation for having shared my books with me from the beginning, for giving me the confidence to write what I do and, most of all, for being my friend.

ISBN 0-373-12080-X

BRIDE OF HIS CHOICE

First North American Publication 2000.

Copyright © 1999 by Emma Darcy.

Visit us at www.romance.net

Printed in U.S.A.

CHAPTER ONE

THE plane touched down with barely a bump. Leigh Durant unclenched her hands and opened her eyes. She was back. A safe landing…though the nerves still knotted in her stomach proclaimed there was little else that would be *safe* about this trip.

From her seat next to a window, she noted the rain forecast for Sydney was certainly accurate. The view of Botany Bay was obliterated by wet darkness.

It was a dark and stormy night…

The cartoon character Snoopy, sitting on his doghouse with his typewriter, always started his stories with those ominous words. Leigh wondered if she was starting a new phase of her life by coming home or simply ending the one that had started the day she was born, twenty-four years ago.

Ever since the media had broken the news of Lawrence Durant's fatal heart attack, she'd started hoping her long, lonely exile was over. Yet she wasn't sure of anything where her family was concerned. All she knew was the man who had so cruelly dominated their lives was dead. And Leigh wanted to see him buried. Buried beyond any possible redemption. After that…

Well, she'd try to ascertain if it was possible to forge a new relationship with her mother and sisters. They might not want anything to do with her. It had been six years since she'd been part of their world…six years since she'd run away from the hell of knowing she didn't belong to it and never could while ever Lawrence Durant lived. It might be that none of them would welcome her back...and the hole of emptiness in her life would never be filled.

Leigh instinctively fought against the prospect of that bleak outcome. There had to be a chance. Lawrence was no longer there to influence their behaviour towards her...the daughter who wasn't *his* daughter, the cuckoo he'd hated having in his nest. Her mother and sisters were free of him now. Surely she could be re-united with them, if there was any fairness at all in this world.

The plane came to a halt. Leigh released her seat-belt and rose with the other passengers to retrieve her hand luggage. She was stiff and tired and did a bit of stretching to ease her cramped muscles as they waited in line to disembark. It had been a long trip—yesterday's flight from Broome to Perth, the stopover there to buy suitable clothes, then this afternoon's flight from Perth to Sydney, right across the Australian continent. It would be good just to get out of the plane.

The passengers moved slowly down the aisle towards the exit door. Leigh had worked her way up to being level with the first-class seats when her gaze fell on a discarded newspaper. The photograph of a face caught her eye and her heart contracted.

Richard...Richard Seymour.

Before she even realised what she was doing, the newspaper was in her hand and she was staring at the current image of the man who'd haunted her teenage years.

"Move on!" someone called impatiently.

"You're holding us up, Miss," the man behind her said more politely.

"Sorry," she gabbled, her face burning as she hurried forward and shot into the disembarking tunnel, still holding the wretched newspaper. She wished she could drop it and vowed to do so the moment she reached the first litter bin inside the terminal.

Richard Seymour...

She'd read about him in various articles relating to Lawrence Durant's shock death...the man who was now in charge of the vast financial empire, steadying the ripples on the stock exchange...the man groomed by the great tycoon to take over from him...Lawrence Durant's protégé and right hand. But none of the articles had been accompanied by a photograph.

It was seeing his face again that had got to her, releasing a flood of the ambivalent feelings he'd always stirred. Stupid! she savagely berated herself. One thing was certain. If this was the start of a new phase in her life, *he* wouldn't be featuring in it. There was no reason for him to ever mix with the Durant family again. He now had what he wanted, the top spot with no one to answer to except the shareholders.

A furious energy coursed through her as she entered the airport terminal, spotted a rubbish bin and strode straight over to it, ridding herself of the photographic reminder of a man who wasn't worth thinking about. Of course she would see him at the funeral tomorrow. Richard Seymour could hardly miss that. But no-one could force her to have anything to do with him. Not any more. Lawrence Durant was dead.

It was still raining when she stepped out of the terminal. Luckily she didn't have to queue for a taxi-cab. There were plenty waiting. She ran to one, jumped into the back seat, hauling her bag with her, shut the door and gave the address of her hotel to the driver. He zipped off into the line of traffic and Leigh tried to relax.

Impossible task. She stared broodingly out at the wet street, a zigzag of lights reflected in sheets of streaming water. *A dark and stormy night*...was it an omen? Should she have stayed in Broome, keeping the past pushed behind her? Was she on a totally hopeless mission?

No point in not going through with it now, she stubbornly reasoned. She was here. Tomorrow she would go to Lawrence Durant's funeral, see her mother and sisters, and their attitude towards her would determine if she had a place here or not. One day was probably all it would take to settle her future course. At the very least, she wouldn't be left wondering for the rest of her life.

CHAPTER TWO

NOTHING had changed…

Leigh stood in the grand reception room of the Durant mansion, feeling the same oppressive sense of being utterly worthless as she had as a teenager, as a child. It was as though she'd moved back in time and all she had escaped from was swamping her again; the insecurities, the rejections, the fear of not fitting in, the despair of not belonging.

It should be different now, she fiercely told herself. Lawrence Durant—*her father* for the first eighteen years of her life—was dead. Surely his repressive, tyrannical force had died with him, leaving her mother and sisters free to follow their own inclinations instead of kowtowing to his rule. Was it too soon for them to realise he was truly gone? Hadn't the funeral today brought that home to them?

Conversation at the chapel service had naturally been limited. The shock of seeing her after so long an absence might have caused a loss of words, too, but why were they avoiding her now, ignoring her presence, leaving her completely alone? If they would only show her a glimmer of welcome…

Feeling hopelessly ill at ease amongst the crowd of notable people who filled the reception room, paying their last respects to a man who'd wielded wealth and power, Leigh felt a jab of hopeful relief on seeing her mother detach herself from one mourners' group and move away, unaccompanied. She moved quickly to intercept her, touching her arm to draw attention.

"Mother?"

Alicia Durant shot her youngest daughter a brief, impatient glance. "Not now, Leigh. I must get back to Richard."

It was the barest pause, a frowning acknowledgement, so devoid of warmth it made Leigh shrivel inside. She dropped her hand and watched with a sense of wretched helplessness as her mother made a beeline towards the man who already had the undivided attention of her four sisters.

Richard Seymour...the heir apparent of Lawrence Durant's financial empire, presiding over the great tycoon's funeral and this ostentatious wake in the family mansion. She'd refused to even glance at him at the funeral. Looking at him now brought an instant resurgence of her old hatred of him.

He was still everything she wasn't and never could be...what Lawrence Durant had wanted of his fifth child...the shining son to carry on from him. Except the fifth child his wife had delivered was Leigh, another daughter by another man, a total reject who'd never shown any attributes worth the slightest bit of notice, apart from disapproving notice. Cruel notice when comparisons were made to Richard Seymour, the chosen one.

He certainly shone in every department—looks, brains, personal charisma. The aura of power and success and confident purpose literally pulsed from him. Leigh deliberately turned her back on him, telling herself none of this mattered any more. She no longer had any reason to hate Richard Seymour. She'd made her own life away from everything Lawrence Durant had ever touched, and had only come to his funeral out of a sense of closure to that miserable part of her life.

And to see if she meant anything to the rest of her family...her mother and sisters.

It was self-defeating to let these old feelings get to her today. She no longer wished to be something she wasn't. It had taken her a long time to become her own person—six struggling, lonely years—and Richard Seymour could not affect that now. If she could just show her family that she'd come of age, more or less, and that things could be different...

Leigh heaved a sigh to relieve the painful tightness in her chest. Her mother and sisters were probably dancing attendance on Richard Seymour out of habit. The king is dead. Long live the king. Except Richard was not family, so Leigh didn't really understand their fixation on him. He couldn't rule their lives as Lawrence Durant had. Not with the same iron hand and surely not with the same cruel judgement of crime and punishment.

Maybe when the wake was over and all these people who had to be impressed were gone, there would be a better opportunity to re-unite with her family. She'd give it a chance anyhow, one concerted effort to mend the bridges she'd broken in fleeing from the unbearable existence she'd led in this house.

Meanwhile, there seemed little point and no pleasure in hanging around the edges of this crowd, forced to chat to people who could only see her as a curiosity. She made her way out to the back patio which was not in use, due to a gusty wind which would undoubtedly discomfort most guests.

It didn't worry Leigh. She wasn't wearing a hat and she didn't have a fancy hairstyle that could be ruined.

The thick mass of her almost waist-length hair could be untangled with a brush when she went back inside.

She wandered over to the steps leading down to the gardens which were terraced to the water's edge, and paused to look out over the much prized vista of Sydney Harbour. Last night's rain had gone but it was a grey winter day, no warmth or sparkle anywhere. Even the boats seemed to be hurrying to get to their destination.

She thought of the seaport of Broome, high up on the coast of the other side of Australia where there was constant heat, turquoise waters, and "hurry" was a foreign word—a different life a long way from this city. But had she really made her home there or was it still a refuge?

"Leigh…"

Her head jerked around at the unexpected call of her name. Nerves already shredded by being virtually ignored by her family were instantly on edge. Richard… Richard Seymour…seeking her out for attention? He was so closely entwined with Lawrence Durant in her mind, fear clutched at her heart, making it skitter until defiance surged to the fore.

She wasn't a teenager trapped in this place any more. She was an independent young woman, twenty-four years old and well established in another life away from here. There was nothing she could be threatened with, nothing anyone could hold over her head, and she'd learnt to cope with all manner of things.

She stood tall and straight and still, forcing herself to stare coolly at the man who had been a figure of torment to her in the past. Her mind was a total blank on why he'd bother with her at this point in time. What business with or interest in the black sheep of the Durant family could he possibly have?

Not once in the past six years had she asked for or tried to claim a single thing from the Durant holdings. So why on earth would Richard Seymour leave his admirers and follow her out here? She had to be totally irrelevant to his life.

"...you're not leaving, are you?" he demanded more than inquired.

He looked concerned, which confused Leigh even more. "Why would you care?" she asked in bewilderment.

He strolled towards her, a whimsical appeal in the smile he constructed for her. "I haven't had a chance to talk to you."

Leigh instinctively bristled at the projection of charm. He hadn't attempted to charm her in the past. Why now? What was the point? "I wasn't aware we had anything to talk about," she blurted out.

It didn't stop him. Her nerves screwed up another notch. She didn't want him with her. He brought back too many memories...painful, bitter memories of hopes dashed and dreams turned to dust.

"You've been gone a long time," he remarked casually as he closed the distance between them, making her very conscious of how tall and aggressively male he was.

The perfect tailoring of his dark mourning suit gave him a polished veneer but Leigh wasn't fooled by it. Richard Seymour was a hunter in the same mould as Lawrence Durant. For some obscure reason he was hunting her at the moment and her heart was quivering, still reacting to the old fear of being pounced upon.

Somehow, she summoned up an ironic smile. "Did

you want to welcome me home?'' No one else had and she certainly didn't expect him to.

He was quite sickeningly handsome up close. The photograph in the newspaper hadn't done him justice, missing the compelling vitality he'd always emitted. He had to be thirty-four now and definitely in his prime. His clear tanned skin gave his face a healthy glow. His hair, not quite as black as hers, had an attractive wave which some hairstylist had made the most of. His nose was strong and straight and his mouth perfectly balanced. Although his jaw line was rather squarish, the firmly defined chin lent even more strength to his features.

Despite all this impressive framework, it was his eyes that drew and dominated, piercing blue eyes, all the more compelling for being set off by thick black lashes and arched eyebrows which carried more than a hint of arrogance. They scanned her expression with too sharp an intelligence for Leigh's comfort.

"Have you come home?'' he asked in a soft lilt that sent a shiver down her spine.

All the defences she could summon shot into place. He was not going to get to her. She couldn't—wouldn't—let him. With the most determined deliberation Leigh could manage, she adopted a careless air.

"Only to test the waters again. They seem rather cold at the moment so I thought I'd take a walk in the garden while the VIPs are attended to.'' She threw him a dismissive little smile as she added, "If you'll excuse me…'' then proceeded down the steps.

His voice followed her. "Do you mind if I accompany you?''

It wasn't so much a shiver this time. Her spine literally crawled with a tangled mass of unresolved feelings, but nothing good could come of pursuing any of them with Richard Seymour. That time was gone...gone... gone! He might look like hero material but he hadn't been a hero when it counted to her, when she'd wished he'd charge in like a white knight, smiting her father and rescuing her. Such foolish, teenage yearnings!

She squared her shoulders before glancing back at him. "You'll be missed," she pointed out, mocking the importance everyone else placed on his company.

"You're the person I want to be with," he said with a directness that jiggled something deep in Leigh's heart, deep and dangerous to her.

"Not a good choice," she quickly parried.

"It's mine. I don't allow other people to make my choices for me."

There was purpose written in his eyes, undivertable purpose. As much as Leigh wanted to defy it, she knew he would not be turned away. A ruthless hunter always caught up with what he was hunting.

Did he think she'd come home to make trouble for him? Did he see her as someone he might need to pin down and neutralise so his takeover from Lawrence Durant was absolutely smooth? A black sheep could be unpredictable. After all, why turn up at the funeral after six years of non-communication?

Knowing herself to be a total waste of Richard Seymour's time, Leigh decided no harm could come to her from one brief cross-examination from him. "Fine!" she agreed, then, determined to show she wasn't disturbed by the prospect, she added, "I do admire people who have the strength of character to make their own choices."

He smiled. "So do I."

Leigh felt a very definite punch to the heart. His smile seemed to link her to him, as though they were co-conspirators in complete tune with each other. Leigh instantly rejected the idea, but she still felt shaken by it. Richard Seymour was not the man she'd wanted him to be and she wasn't about to be tricked into thinking differently.

He ran appreciative eyes over her as he headed down the steps. "You're looking good, Leigh."

"Thank you." She dragged out the memory of the last time he'd commented on her appearance, instinctively defending herself against the flattering power of his compliment. "As opposed to looking anorexic, I presume."

He'd accused her of it after one of Lawrence's ritual Sunday lunches, which she'd been unable to eat, her stomach too screwed up to accept anything. Although she had been dieting, her non-consumption of that meal had nothing to do with losing weight.

Richard shrugged. "Believe it or not, I was worried about you at the time. You were far too thin."

"And you put it so kindly. *Anorexia might be a way of taking control of your body but it won't give you control over anything else*," she quoted.

His eyes locked onto hers again as he reached her side at the foot of the steps. "I thought you needed a jolt," he explained without apology.

He was giving her a jolt right now with his perverse interest in her, with the clarity of a memory that surely held no significance to him. She'd been seventeen, fighting what she then saw as an unfair weight problem, trying to look more like her model-slim sisters. Impossible task.

She'd been born with a different bone structure and no matter how thin she got, the natural curves of her body denied her a boyish figure. Away from the repressive influences of her family, she'd grown into the woman she was always going to be, voluptuously curved, but not grossly so for her height. She was taller than average, though even in high heels, she found herself half a head shorter than Richard Seymour, looking up to him, which she suddenly resented.

"Well, Richard," she drawled, turning away to start down the path to the ornamental pond, "let me tell you I don't need your approval for who or what I am. In fact, your opinion—good or bad—is irrelevant to me." Which put him in his place in *her* world.

He laughed as he fell into step with her.

Leigh found herself clenching her hands at his amusement. She sliced him a totally unamused look, wishing he would take his disturbing presence elsewhere.

He grinned. "I have missed the black blaze of those incredibly expressive eyes."

Missed? Had she really made such a strong impression on him all those years ago? Or was he attempting to flirt with her, now that she "looked good"?

She frowned over the questions as he walked on with her. The black suit she'd bought for the funeral was figure-hugging. She didn't favour layers of shapeless clothes that made her look fat. Apparently Richard liked her current shape. As for her eyes, Leigh simply accepted them as part and parcel of her coloring—matching the blackness of her hair and toning with her olive skin. She had a slightly long nose and a wide, very full-

lipped mouth, and she'd come to accept them, too. Since
her face had filled out, the features she'd despaired over
looked more right somehow, in keeping with the rest of
her.

Certainly she no longer felt like *the ugly duckling*
she'd always been in the Durant household, though she
could never be counted as a blonde beauty like her older
sisters. Ruefully she remembered her one desperate attempt to dye her hair blonde. Total disaster. Like everything else she had attempted in her teens in her hopeless
need to fit some acceptable mould. She hadn't known
then she was a cuckoo in the nest and cuckoos couldn't
turn into anything else.

"I have no doubt you have no need of *my* approval,
Leigh," Richard picked up, apparently determined on
teasing her out of her silence. As she glanced at him he
added, "There wouldn't be one red-blooded male who
didn't approve of you."

Sex! Leigh wrenched her gaze from his and walked
faster, inwardly fuming over this shallow view of her.
She was more than just a lush body that a lot of men
fancied. But then men like Richard Seymour probably
didn't want a woman with a mind or a heart. Taking sex
as needed was probably his style.

In all the publicity and media speculation sparked by
Lawrence Durant's fatal heart attack, the newspapers had
made much of the fact Richard Seymour was not married—one of the most eligible bachelors in Australia—
and Leigh wondered if he was as much a womaniser as
Lawrence Durant had been, behind the respectable fa-
cade of his marriage. With his looks, Richard certainly
wouldn't lack choice.

Was he now thinking the same of her? He was wrong,

if he did. She hadn't even cared to sample the chances that had come her way. Somehow an internal barrier went up the moment any man started getting too close to her. As for desiring them...she'd often wondered if desire was linked to trust and that was why she couldn't feel it. Maybe one day she would meet someone she could really trust to love her as she wanted to be loved.

"Are you happy in the life you've made for yourself?"

The apparently artless question snapped Leigh out of her private reverie. Danger signals flared in her mind. Give anything away to a man like Richard Seymour and somehow he'd use it against her. She'd had too much experience of that process in the Durant household to be offering any information about herself.

Keeping her *expressive* eyes fixed on the path ahead she answered, "Reasonably," in an even tone, then turned the question back on him. "What about you? Are you happy with what you've made of yourself?"

He laughed again, though there was more irony than amusement in the sound this time. "You know, no-one's ever asked me that question."

Of course. Brilliant success didn't exactly invite any such doubt. "Perhaps you should ask it of yourself?" she drily remarked.

"Perhaps I should," he agreed even more drily. "Though I can't say it's ever been on my list of priorities. I've always thought happiness an elusive thing, not easily captured and even more difficult to hold."

Unlike wealth and power.

"Then why ask me about it?"

"Oh, I guess I was really asking if you've found a relationship you find satisfying."

He dropped the question so casually, the impact came in slow motion. Leigh's first reaction was it was none of his business. Then his previous comment about the approval of "red-blooded men" started to rattle her. Did he fancy a quick fling with her while she was in Sydney? Was this why he'd followed her out here...to ascertain availability and charm his way into her bed? Did he see her as old enough for him now?

The idea was outrageous, yet oddly tantalising. Leigh was tempted to play him along, just to see if it was true. "No, I haven't. At least, not as satisfying as I would wish," she answered honestly, then slid him an assessing look as she added, "But I didn't come home for you, Richard."

It was a mistake to look at him. He instantly locked onto it with a piercing intensity that pinned her eyes to his. "Am I not one of the ghosts you wish to lay to rest?"

"Why would you think so?" she retaliated, disturbed by the wild quickening of her pulse.

"Because you hated me so much."

He was raising the ghosts, deliberately and too evocatively for Leigh's comfort. "Wouldn't you, in my place?" she snapped.

"Yes. But there was nothing I could do to change your place, Leigh. You had to do it yourself. Which you did. Yet I wonder if all those negative feelings towards me—the bitter resentment and the black contempt—still linger on?"

He *was* getting to her, digging around in her head and heart, and she didn't want him to. Realising she'd paused to counter this attack on her feelings, Leigh got her legs moving again, chiding herself for falling into the trap of letting him focus the conversation on her. She tried to switch it back on him.

"I can't imagine it matters to you."

"It does. Very much."

"Why?" she demanded, inwardly refusing to believe him. She would not—*not*—allow herself to be vulnerable to what Richard Seymour thought or felt about her. She'd been down that painful track, wanting *him to shine* for her, but he hadn't.

"I wasn't your enemy," he answered simply. "Your hatred was blind, Leigh. As much as I could be, I was your friend."

Hardly *a friend*, she thought with a violence that startled her. Let it go, she berated herself furiously. Just let it go and set him aside, right out of your life.

"I don't view you as an enemy, Richard," she said as dispassionately as she could. "I don't think I did then, either. Not personally. If you hadn't been the favoured protégé, someone else would have won that place, and been used in the same way to show off my father's dissatisfaction with me."

"I didn't enjoy my place in that particular game, Leigh."

She couldn't stop herself from seething over how he had conducted himself, even though he might not have enjoyed it. "You didn't walk away from it," she tersely remarked.

"As you say, it wouldn't have changed anything," he answered easily. "Lawrence would have found someone else. Someone who might have joined in the game with him, making it worse for you."

In all fairness, she couldn't accuse Richard of aiding or abetting the cruel baiting that had gone on during the mandatory-attendance Sunday luncheons in the Durant mansion. She remembered him diverting the conversation into other topics, taking the focus off her, but she'd hated him for that, too, feeling he pitied her.

She'd wanted him—willed him—to stand up and fight for her, though Lawrence would never have tolerated that from him. With an older, wiser head on her shoulders, she could see that now, but at the time...

She took a deep breath, trying to clear herself of the burning turmoil Richard Seymour could still stir. Applying cold hard reason, it was possible to agree with his point of view. He may well have meant to be *a friend* to her, as much as he could, within the parameters of retaining his position.

"Well, thank you for thinking of my feelings," she said, trying to be fair and wanting this highly unwelcome contretemps finished with. "As it happens, I don't hate you any more, and you're not a ghost I need to lay to rest."

"Good!" He sounded relieved.

His response nagged at Leigh. Why did he care what she felt? Unless, of course, he did want to bed her, and ghosts wouldn't be good in that scenario. But was that really likely? She was no longer sure what was likely with him. He kept on walking with her, seemingly deep in thought, and she couldn't shake the feeling all his thoughts were focused on her.

They reached the ornamental pond. Wanting to reduce any sense of gathering intimacy with a man she could have nothing in common with beyond the memories of imprisoned hours together in the long-ago past, she sat down on the wide sandstone blocks which formed a flat platform on top of the pond's circular enclosure and trailed her fingers through the water, making the fish dart into flashing movement, their luminous colours catching the light.

So beautiful, Leigh thought. Did they know they were prisoners, bought by the wealth of Lawrence Durant for his casual pleasure? Would freedom mean anything to these fish, or would they be lost in a world beyond this confinement? They were well fed, but being well fed wasn't everything. It was good to feel free. Yet even away from this place and all it represented, Leigh knew she was still emotionally tied to it, which was why she'd come back, hoping for...what?

It looked like she was only messing herself up again.

"I'm glad you came back, Leigh."

The soft intonation made the comment sound very, very personal. Leigh instantly steeled herself against its warming effect. If she started wanting too much from Richard Seymour, bitter disillusionment would surely follow. Any closeness with him had to be dangerous. As it was, she was acutely aware of him standing barely a metre away. That distance didn't feel far enough.

"I needed to be here today," she answered flatly, still watching the fish. "The funeral made Lawrence's death real...the coffin...the cremation...ashes to ashes, dust to dust. He doesn't have the power to hurt me any more." *And I won't let you do it, either,* she added resolutely.

"Your mother and sisters...from what I saw, none of them ever stood up for you. Do you expect that to be different now?" he asked, the soft tone projecting a caring she wouldn't let herself believe.

He hadn't stood up, either, though Leigh had to concede he had done more than the others to stop Lawrence's games. On the other hand, as an outsider, he hadn't been personally subjected to them. She wasn't the only one in the family who'd suffered verbal abuse. It had a repressive effect on all of them.

"I don't know if it will be different," she answered honestly. Suddenly and fiercely wishing for some open honesty from him, she lifted her gaze for direct confrontation. "Lawrence pulled the strings then. It looks like you pull them now. So what do you want, Richard? What is this conversation about? You'll do much better with me if you don't play games."

He cocked his head slightly, assessing the strength of that statement. His eyes held no warmth whatsoever. They were coldly calculating and Leigh sensed a ruthless gathering of purpose. When he spoke, there was no preamble, no dressing up with persuasive intent, just the bare bones of what he'd been leading to from the very beginning of this encounter.

"I want to marry you, Leigh."

CHAPTER THREE

LEIGH stared at Richard Seymour, too stunned to really believe her ears, but her eyes didn't pick up any messages that changed what she'd thought she'd heard.

He was watching her with intense concentration, waiting to weigh her reaction. His body looked relaxed but she could feel tension emanating from him. More than tension. Will-power was beaming out of those compelling blue eyes, asserting absolutely serious intent and firming up the wobbly ground inside her mind.

There was only one question to ask so she asked it. "*Why?* Of all the women you could choose to marry, why *me*?"

His mouth curved into a half-smile. "I could give you many reasons, Leigh, but since they're mostly from my point of view, I doubt you'd see them as valid."

Valid!

She laughed. Couldn't help herself. The situation was so wildly improbable, a sense of sheer hysteria bubbled out of her. King Richard wanting Cinderella as his wife? It might be understandable if he was madly in love with her, but that idea was as far-fetched as his proposition.

Leigh couldn't resist pursuing it, her eyes dancing a challenge as she asked, "Just give me one of those reasons, Richard. One I might be able to believe in."

His eyes seemed to twinkle knowingly at her as he said, "We're fellow travellers on a road that started a long time ago. Who else will understand what went into the journey?''

A straight stab to the heart, killing any urge to laugh and instantly evoking a sober and vehement reply. ''I got off that road.''

''Did you?'' he softly challenged. ''Not quite, Leigh, or you would never have come back.''

''I've explained why.''

He nodded. ''I listened, and what I heard is it's not finished for you. You're still seeking...'' He paused a moment, his eyes boring into hers. ''...justice.''

He was crawling into her mind, plucking on heartstrings that did yearn for what had never been given.

''What better justice can there be now than to balance the scales...with you taking all that was taken from you?'' he suggested with a terrible, insidious appeal to the darkness deep inside her. ''I can give it to you, Leigh.''

She wanted to look away, to escape this awful intrusion into her private soul, yet if she did, he would know he had hit truly and the vulnerability was there to be played upon. The darkness was not good. She'd tried to escape it, hating how it blighted her life. She realised now she had come back to confront it, make it go away. But how could marrying him turn it around? Wouldn't it be more of the same?

She'd been right about not giving him information to use against her. He was too clever at reading it. He wouldn't have succeeded Lawrence Durant if he wasn't both diabolically clever and ruthless. And she hadn't forgotten how the game was played. Hiding the hurt defeated the victory. She kept her gaze firmly on his and turned the darkness back onto him.

"Let's cut to the real point, Richard. I don't believe you *want* to marry me, so marriage to me has to have a purpose. What advantage is there in it for you?"

He laughed, completely disarming her for a moment, and his eyes danced at her in open admiration, disarming her even further. "I don't suppose you'd believe me if I said I love you," he tossed at her, moving closer to the sandstone rim of the pond, then lifting a foot onto it, leaning forward, resting his arms on the bent knee.

The pose brought him effectively closer to her, setting up an intimate togetherness while still respecting her personal space. And suddenly there was a sizzle in his eyes that set all her nerve ends twitching.

"But don't think I don't *want* you, Leigh," he said in a low purring voice, stirring even more havoc inside her. "There's nothing about you I don't want, including your blazing directness, which I find more refreshing than you could ever begin to believe."

Her heart was pumping so hard she couldn't think of a word to say. Her mind was jammed with sexual signals. And the terrible part was she couldn't push them out. There was a dreadful fascination in this crazy physical response to Richard Seymour. She remembered how his presence had always tied her in knots when she was a teenager. She hadn't recognised it then as sexual attraction. But now...

Did he know?

Did he *feel* it?

Sheer panic kept her silent.

He was not the least bit perturbed by her lack of response. He went on talking with easy confidence, knowing that she understood what he was spelling out. "You were supposed to be the son to carry on Lawrence's name and dynasty. And you paid one hell of a price for not being that son. What you don't know—yet—is he never lost the obsession of having his own flesh and blood carry on from him.''

''But that's impossible now,'' Leigh murmured, struggling out of her distraction.

''No, it's not impossible…if he has a grandson with the right capabilities. And Lawrence thought of that before he died. Thought of it and planned it.''

A grandson! It was sickening. An innocent little baby boy created for Lawrence Durant's massive ego, life and goals all rigidly mapped out before he even started living. As hers would have been if she had been the right sex and the right material for moulding into the right monument to a man who didn't deserve any kind of monument.

''Did he pick out the name, too?'' she asked in savage disgust. ''Mine was supposed to be Leigh Jason. The Jason part was dropped when I turned out to be a girl.''

''Lawrence,'' came the dry reply.

''Of course. One Lawrence gone. Another coming up.''

Something infinitely dangerous and determined flashed through the clear blue of his eyes. ''He can't reach that far from the grave, Leigh, and his purpose can be defeated.''

She was tantalised by the brief glimpse of something she didn't know—a force driving him that went beyond her previous judgement of his character. ''Go on,'' she urged.

''I was the one who took your designated role, insofar as I met the expectations he would have had for his son. My much publicised position as his successor is not ironclad. It is provisional to my fulfilling the terms of his will.''

"Which are?" she prompted when he paused, although she could guess what was coming, and another painful emptiness yawned inside her.

His mouth curled into a mirthless smile. "If I marry one of his daughters and produce a son, I get the necessary percentage of company shares which will make my position as his successor unassailable."

The right material wedded to the Durant genes.

Hence the proposal of marriage.

Except she couldn't be the chosen one...never the chosen one.

There was one huge flaw in Richard Seymour's selection of her as his bride, and Leigh wasn't the only one who knew it. Her mother certainly did. Her four sisters might very well be aware of it, as well. They'd tell him soon enough, if it served their interests, and the evidence of her own observations pointed that way.

All five of them undoubtedly knew the contents of the will. Whomever Richard chose to marry would be sitting pretty in the world they knew. It explained why her mother and sisters had been so focused on courting his favour and not paying any attention to the return of the prodigal daughter. It was the same old sick game, sucking up to power.

Leigh found her gaze had dropped to the leg Richard had propped on the sandstone platform. The fine woollen fabric of his suit trousers was pulled taut over a strongly muscled thigh. Her mind fuzzed over an image of how he might look naked, all that male power energised by desire, wanting her...

Another fanciful dream turned to dust, she thought,

feeling the same old ache of disappointment Richard had always left her with. If she told him the truth he wouldn't want her, not as a wife. Even if he still fancied her— the woman she was now—she couldn't allow anything to come of it, knowing he would inevitably choose to make one of her sisters his bride. Best to cut it dead right now.

She dragged her gaze up and kept it levelled on his as she delivered her rejection. "The answer is no, Richard. I won't marry you."

Then to emphasise the matter was closed, she was up on her feet with her back turned to him and heading towards the steps that led down to the next terrace, away from him, away from the house that had dominated much of her life, away from the family who cared more for what it represented than they'd ever cared for her.

"Why not?" Richard shot after her.

She waved a dismissive hand without glancing around. "You have four other daughters to choose from. You just struck out on me, that's all."

"I don't *want* any of the others," he declared vehemently.

She shook her head over the black irony of that statement and kept on walking, down the steps to the summer-house which presided over the terrace of rose gardens. She could hear his footsteps following her and fiercely wished he'd leave her alone.

It was so perverse of him to choose her ahead of the far more suitable daughters, the beautiful blonde accomplished socialites with the right blood in them, only too eager to snap him up and grace his arm, his bed, and his bank balance. Felicity, Vanessa, Caroline, Nadine...such pretty, feminine, classy names.

The impulse to shove one truth she'd had to accept down Richard Seymour's throat made Leigh pause by the summer-house and cast a derisive look at him. He was already at the foot of the steps and striding towards her.

"You know, Richard, most people don't get everything they want. You may not be used to that but I'm sure compromises sometimes have to be taken, even in your world."

He kept on coming. "You can have everything you want from me, Leigh."

The strong conviction in his voice clutched at her heart, but only for a moment. He wasn't offering love. He probably didn't know what love was, any more than she did. The sheer sweep of his extravagant promise suddenly evoked another wild laugh, peeling into a wind that carried it away from her as swiftly as it arose.

It didn't stop him. His eyes didn't waver from hers, determined on burning away her scorn and supplanting it with possibilities that could breed hope. But there *was* no hope.

"It's very simple, Richard," she said flatly. "Regardless of what you can give me, I can't give *you* what you want."

He came to a halt, barely a metre away, totally unperturbed by her claim. His eyes challenged it with ruthless intent as he said, "Because you're not Lawrence Durant's daughter?"

Shock reverberated through her. "You know?" The words spilled from her lips before she could catch them back. Had he guessed or had he pushed her into admission? His proposal made no sense if he *knew*. A churning turmoil of shame and pride robbed her of any movement as he stepped towards her, a mesmerising satisfaction written on his face.

"I knew the day I first met you, Leigh. You didn't belong to Lawrence, not physically, not mentally, not emotionally. No bond at all and nothing of him in you. Nothing."

It wasn't proof, she thought, but he went on, shattering that thought.

"Lawrence confirmed it when you went away and I suggested someone should be hired to keep track of you in case you were in need. 'She's my wife's child, not mine!' was what he said, then swore me to silence on the subject. A proud man like Lawrence didn't care to have it known that you weren't his."

The power of his total self-assurance held her still, though her heart was pounding wildly and tremors of shock were still running through her.

"Legally, you are his."

"No." Her voice sounded hollow but the words had to be said now. "He disinherited me when I left."

"He made no provision for you in his will, Leigh, but nowhere is there a claim that denies you are his child. And since Lawrence was cremated today, there can be no DNA tests to prove you aren't. I can marry you in good faith with the terms of his will."

Instinctively she fought against the relentless beat of his logic. "My mother could name my real father."

A grim little smile curled his mouth. "It's not in her best interests to do so."

The manipulation of wealth! Leigh's hatred of it spurred her to argue. "What makes you think my real father wouldn't come forward if he saw money in it?"

That killed the smile. Yet, even more disturbing, his

eyes seemed to soften with sympathy. "It won't happen, Leigh," he said quietly. "Your mother paid for him and his family to go back to Italy before you were born. From the date of their departure, I'd say he knows nothing of you."

"Go back to Italy?" she picked up in bewilderment.

"You didn't know he was Italian?"

She shook her head. On the terrible night she had learnt Lawrence Durant was not her father, her mother had refused to reveal the true circumstances of her birth. The argument between Lawrence and his wife had raged over her head, and had more to do with financial arrangements than the infidelity that had brought her into their world. They had forgotten her in hurling threats at one another. She'd simply slipped away, packed her things and left.

Italian...well, that explained her colouring. There weren't too many blonde Italians. It probably explained her non-boyish figure, as well. The only Italian actress she could think of was Sophia Loren, whose curvaceous femininity was legendary. Leigh supposed a hot-blooded Italian lover would have made a tempting contrast to Lawrence Durant, but her mother had hardly been wise in having a child by him, risking the possibility of producing the cuckoo Leigh had turned out to be.

"He was the gardener here at the time of your conception," Richard explained.

It shocked her into speech. "A gardener? My mother took a gardener as her lover?" It seemed unbelievable. Her mother was a dyed-in-the-wool snob who invariably disdained to notice what she considered the lower classes.

"He had four sons, Leigh."

Ah…the logic of it was instantly crystal clear. No escaping *that* connection. A man who fathered sons was precisely what was wanted when four daughters had been delivered and a son was required.

Leigh closed her eyes, revolted by the calculation that had gone into her conception…the payment that had been made for a service rendered. No doubt, if there'd been ultrasound scans done all those years ago to determine the sex of the baby, the pregnancy would have been terminated and she wouldn't even be alive today. Her mother had probably gambled on having a child that took after her in looks and colouring. No wonder she'd been *unwanted*. She represented failure in every sense.

"How do you know all this, Richard?" she asked, raising lashes that felt unnaturally heavy, but needing to see the answer in his eyes.

"I made it my business to find out."

"Why?" A weary, aching cynicism prompted her to add, "To ensure there was no wild card that could upset your plan?"

"There was no plan when I set about getting the information. That was six years ago, Leigh."

She frowned, realising the terms of the will would only have been revealed on Lawrence's death. "Then what use was it to you?"

His serious expression was softened by a touch of whimsy. "Oh, I thought one day you might like to know who your real father is."

"You did it for me?" She shook her head incredulously, unable to believe such altruism from a man who clearly calculated everything.

"We have more in common than you think," he said wryly. "I was not the child of the man my mother was married to. I bear his name but I'm not his child, and I knew it very early on.''

Leigh was dumbfounded. There'd never been a whisper of anything scandalous in his background. Another private family secret? Then it burst upon her that he knew what it felt like...travelling the same road...and he'd seen it all along in her...a fellow traveller.

"The truth of such a situation is not easy to deal with and a name can become important," he went on. "Your father's name is Mario Vangelli. He and his family live in Naples. I can give you the address should you ever want to visit."

Vangelli...Richard was right. It *was* good to have a name instead of a blank. "What about you?" She eyed him curiously. "Did you find your real father?"

"Yes. He was married to someone else. They had a family. He didn't know I was his son and I didn't tell him." His expression hardened. "As with your father, it was just seed sown that he walked away from."

Paid to walk away from in her case. "I wouldn't feel right about visiting, but thank you for telling me about him, Richard. It is better knowing than not knowing."

He nodded, an understanding in his eyes that shared the scars of being a bastard child who didn't belong to the marriage of either parents.

"I might never have come back," she mused. "You might have got that information for nothing, Richard."

He shook his head. "Information is always useful."

Cynicism returned in a swift bitter sweep. It was information he could have used against her mother, or Lawrence, for that matter. "Of course," she drawled. "Knowledge is power."

"And you were always going to come back," he continued without so much as a ripple in his cast-iron confidence. "When you felt ready to."

"Lucky for you it was now or you would have had no choice but to propose to one of my sisters," she mocked.

"Luck has nothing to do with it. If you hadn't come I would have gone to you."

Her heart contracted. He really did want *her* above the others. "You would have had to track me down," she pointed out.

"I've kept track of you all along, Leigh. As soon as I knew you had gone, I acted to ensure you were safe, and stayed safe, wherever you went and whatever you did. There wasn't one day of these past six years that I haven't known where you were, and been assured you were managing by yourself. I knew what flight you took out of Broome, where you stayed in Perth, and what time you arrived in Sydney last night. And I knew you would be here today."

It shook her, more than any of the previous shocks he'd delivered. Or perhaps it was the culminating effect of all of them. "You had someone spying on me?"

"No, not spying. Just checking that you were coping on your own, not in trouble, not in need of help. There was absolutely no interference in your life, Leigh, nor in whatever you chose to do."

"Why did you do it?" she cried, still appalled at having been so comprehensively watched over.

It came again, that brief flash of something deep and dark and dangerous behind the crisp blue of his eyes. "Because I cared. And no one else did." Even his voice carried a note of ferocity, suggestive of feelings he hadn't quite kept under control.

Leigh tried to focus on it but Richard distracted her by moving closer, lifting a hand and touching her cheek, soft fingertips grazing her skin, raising electric tingles. "Think, Leigh," he commanded, the powerful impact of his eyes increased by the knowledge he had of her. "You came, looking for some portion of justice..."

That was true.

"Marry me...and you'll have what your mother sacrificed you for...what your sisters covet. You'll have all that Lawrence denied you and more. What greater justice than to take what you were born for..."

Her head whirled with his words, all of them striking such painful places.

"I hand you the keys to the whole Durant empire, everything Lawrence acquired in his ruthless drive for power..."

To the exile, the spoils, she thought wildly.

"...and no one will scorn you again, Leigh, or treat you in a contemptible manner. As my wife, you will be my queen, in every sense."

As long as I give you a son.

There was always a price for the pot of gold.

"I want you as my queen, Leigh."

The low throb of his voice was like a drumbeat on her heart.

"Only you can satisfy me. Only you. We're two of a kind, Leigh. You and I."

And that mesmerising message blazed from his eyes as he moved closer, an arm sliding around her waist, taking possession, the hand on her face suddenly cupping her chin, holding it tilted, and she knew he was going to kiss her, knew he meant to seduce her to his will, but somehow she didn't want to stop him.

Her entire being was quivering with anticipation.

CHAPTER FOUR

LEIGH held her breath at the first brush of his mouth on hers, the contact so tantalisingly gentle, it took all her concentration to absorb each shift of pleasurable sensation. It wasn't a *taking* kiss. She would have fought it if he'd tried to blitz her with dominant strength. The relief of this controlled exploration allowed her to relax and let the urge to know flow freely.

She had blocked him out all these years, coupling him with Lawrence Durant, yet today she had been forcefully reminded that her hatred of Richard had been fed from the fierce wish for him to act differently. To her teenage mind he'd had the strength to fight her father, to stand up for her, to be her champion, and he hadn't done it. Not how she'd wanted it done, not enough to satisfy the bitter churning of needs inside her.

Could he give her satisfaction now?

Would he?

The feathery caresses teased her into responding, and no sooner had her lips softened and parted than the light pressures changed to a deeper searching, and she felt moving through her a great swell of yearning for the promise of everything...everything she'd ever wanted and could ever want.

Had the normal flow of such feelings been somehow locked up around Richard Seymour? Was this strange shifting inside herself the release of barriers that had

38

been subconciously focused on needs *he* should have fulfilled?

Her mind and body were in such a whirl of inner chaos, she wasn't aware of lifting her arms. The instinct to press closer, to hold on to *this* moment of reckoning, to see it through as far as it went, swept her hands around his neck. His embrace instantly tightened, moulding her body to the hard length of his, and his mouth engaged hers in a far more passionate intimacy, stirring a sensual storm that spread like wildfire.

The heat of it banished the cold emptiness of being unloved and unwanted and ignited a hunger that craved everything she had missed out on. She revelled in the hungry ravishing of her mouth, exulted in every bit of the physical contact, the squashing of her breasts across the muscular breadth of his chest, the exciting pressure of his arousal, the straining of rock-hard thighs against hers. He did *want* her. It felt as though he was reaching out to her with every fibre of his being and the thrill of it was too enthralling to stop.

It was he who broke off the all-consuming flow of desire, suddenly throwing his head back, dragging in air, breathing so hard his chest heaved, bringing a rush of sensitivity to her breasts and stirring an intense frustration at the abrupt halt to what he'd started. She stared at him in confusion, seeing the tension on his face, not understanding anything except he'd stopped kissing her.

He moved the hand he'd curled around her head, touching her sensitised lips, tracing them with his fingers. Her daze cleared enough for her to see the glitter of triumphant satisfaction in his eyes as he spoke.

"It feels right, doesn't it, Leigh? The time has come for *us*."

Control, she thought. He wants to control this to suit him. Just as Lawrence Durant would. Never again would she submit to that. Never! The sweet, warm chaos he'd wrought inside her welded into a savage bolt of rebellion.

He'd run everything *his* way, following her out here, feeding her information, capitalizing on the chemistry between them. Well, she wouldn't let him control this. He wasn't going to mastermind when and how she got to satisfy herself about him.

All these years of spying on her, knowing where she was but not coming to her, waiting for her to come to him, thinking he could manipulate what he wanted of her, pressing buttons he had the power to press…oh, no! It was *her* turn to press the button!

"If it feels so right to you, Richard, what's wrong with *now*?" she challenged.

"You want *now*?"

The flare of raw desire in his eyes shot a turbulent mix of fear and elation through Leigh. What was she inviting, goading from him? The challenge had been a vengeful impulse. She hadn't stopped to think of the ultimate end of what she was laying on him, and he didn't wait for a reply.

He scooped her with him as he stepped to the door of the summer-house, opened it, and whirled her inside. By the time Leigh's feet steadied on the floor, the door was closed and she was pressed against it, and his mouth was delivering another rush of warm pleasure that felt very right, so right she held his head to hers, wanting his kissing to continue, kissing him back in a fierce need to fill herself with the warmth he generated, to keep the cold out.

Tautly muscled thighs lent supportive strength to hers as his hands roamed over her body, their touch hot and excitingly lustful as they felt her curves, reaching around the width of her hips to stroke the round slopes of her bottom, clutching them to press her closer to the source of his heat, the hard thrust of it liquefying her stomach, and he kissed her with all the raw intent of what he wanted, promising it would be all she wanted.

But would it? This had never happened to her before. She didn't know the end, had no experience of it. Maybe it was wrong, but she was caught in a force of her own making and she didn't want to break out of it.

Let him show her. Let him be the one. And if the promise wasn't fulfilled, she'd know then, wouldn't she? So she kissed him back with all the fire he'd lit in taking her this far.

Hands sliding to her waist, spanning it possessively, moving to unbutton her suit coat, parting it, and she was glad she hadn't worn a bra, only the silk teddy softly cupping her breasts, allowing firm palms and fingers to cup them so much more satisfyingly, making them feel lush and incredibly sensual and deliciously desirable.

Fingers sliding under the silk, kneading, caressing, exciting, lifting…then his mouth tore from hers, head swooping down, and she felt the bare peak of her breast hotly enveloped and this was a different kissing, hard suction pumping the most piercing pleasure through her, and her own fingers buried themselves in his hair, tugging and pressing, driving the action on, wanting the exquisite arc of sensation to keep vibrating through her.

She'd never felt anything like this before. Was it him? Was it the raw vulnerability of the day making it more than it would normally be? Was it her…giving up the

fight she'd been fighting all her life, letting sheer reck-
lessness take over? She didn't know and didn't
care…savagely didn't care.

She was barely aware of her skirt being pushed up,
but she felt his hand moving between her legs, making
a space, moving past where her stockings ended to the
bare skin above, to the hot moist apex of her thighs, his
thumb hooking apart the studs that held her teddy in
place.

Then the barrier of silk was gone and his touch made
the arc complete, a touch that echoed the same pulsing
rhythm of his mouth, so that everything inside her quiv-
ered with the need for more and more of this unbelievable feeling.

She was melting. She threw her head back against the
door in a blind seeking for something solid. It knocked
her into opening her eyes, a last snatch at some outside
reality. It was dark in the summer-house, the shutters
closed against the winter wind, making it a secret, private place. No one could see what was happening to her.
She didn't want to see herself, only to feel.

She shut her eyes tight, welcoming the darkness, giving free rein to the darkness inside her, a wild, whirling
chaos that revelled in the sheer wantonness of savouring
all that Richard was doing to her. *Time for us,* he'd said,
but it was really time for her…the first…and maybe the
only time.

And she wanted it. Her whole body was screaming
for absolute fulfilment. A wild, guttural protest burst
from her throat when his mouth released her breast, but
then his lips were covering hers again and his tongue
promised the invasion she craved, and suddenly it wasn't
his hand between her thighs. Something else was sliding

down the intimate folds of her flesh, something hard and strong and purposeful, and every nerve end zinged with a sharp, intense awareness of it.

An arm around her waist, lifting her, swinging her. She clutched his back. Then soft cushioning underneath her and the hot spearing of his flesh, stretching a place that had never been stretched, her hands raking his back, urging him on, a hesitation from him and a hoarse command from her, "Do it!" She didn't want control from him. No control. This was her doing, not his. Her decision, not his.

And he did as she demanded, the brief pain of a barrier broken swallowed up by the fullness of a plunge that reached to the epicentre of need and pinned her to a new explosion of sensation, shock waves of it unfurling, overwhelming all that had gone before, then tide after tide of sweet pleasure with the rush of him filling her, withdrawing, and coming again and again, an ebb and flow that engaged her whole body in the rhythm of a different life where she was not alone, not empty, not set at a distance from everyone else, because *he* was with her, inside her, and she could feel the melding with him in every cell of her body.

And finally, he spilled his strength into her and he could do no more. There was a brief sense of ecstatic harmony before he lifted himself away from her, slowly, carefully, and for some reason she didn't mind the parting, still entranced with the feelings swimming through her, more languorously now, yet warm and lovely and infinitely comforting, because this could never be taken away from her. She had it in her keeping no matter what the future brought.

Her first time…amazingly with a man she'd never believed she'd be intimate with…yet it *had* felt right…with his knowing and understanding so much, the sharing of a past that coloured everything. Richard… Richard Seymour…showing her how it was. Or how it could be between them.

She lifted her lashes enough to see what he was doing. While she still lay in listless abandonment on one of the cane sofas, he'd fixed up his clothes, all very much together again as though nothing untoward had taken place. He opened the camphor chest that served as a table surface beside one of the armchairs, picked out a packet of paper serviettes, broke them open and came back to her, gently padding the tissues and cleaning up the aftermath of her torn virginity.

"Are you hurting, Leigh?" he asked softly.

"No," she answered, struggling to control her inner recoil from what he was doing…so matter-of-fact, almost clinical…bringing her down to earth with a shocking thump. The wild emotional chaos that had led her to this…this messiness…had also robbed her of dignity.

Best to let him get it over with, she argued to herself, fiercely wishing she had lost her virginity in other circumstances. But to whom? Only Richard had made her feel as though it was right. Except now, he was in control again, more in control than ever because she had given him these liberties with her. Somehow she had to stop him from taking a whole lot more because it might not be right at all.

His mouth curved into a self-mocking little smile. "Not quite the way I would have taken my bride, had I known you were a true bride."

"Bride?" Her heart catapulted around her chest. Letting him be the first didn't mean she had to join her whole life to his. "I haven't said I'll marry you, Richard," she quickly reminded him, instinctively fighting any sense of commitment that would give him power over her.

He threw her a dark, intense look. "You will."

She wasn't sure if that was certainty or resolution. He was distracting her, stroking her thighs, making them quiver again. He leaned over and kissed her stomach, a long warm lingering kiss, reminding her of the deep, inner connection that had been forged. But it wasn't the answer to everything, Leigh thought frantically. Not *everything*.

He tugged down her teddy and smoothed her skirt over her nakedness. He bestowed sensual kisses on her breasts, too, before tucking them back in their silk casing. "You are an incredibly beautiful woman, Leigh," he murmured huskily. Then his mouth was on hers, a sweet tingling sealing of a memory...or an assurance this was only a beginning, not an end.

"Ready to move?" he asked.

"No. You go," she urged, desperately needing a break from his company so she could sort out the confusion in her mind. She wasn't sure of anything right now, except she'd done this amazing thing with him and she had to think through the consequences of it.

"Not without you, Leigh," he replied swiftly, determination flashing through the caring in his eyes.

"You're the one who will be missed," she argued, instantly backing away from letting him order her around.

"I want you with me." A categorical statement.

She shook her head, the fear of being manipulated

rushing through her. "I'm not ready to take that stand with you, Richard."

He frowned. "I have no intention of making some public announcement, Leigh. I just want..."

She pressed her fingers to his lips, her inner agitation too great to listen to any more persuasive words. "Let me be," she pleaded. "I want time on my own right now."

He didn't like it. She watched the conflict between purpose and an awareness of moving too far too fast, and saw the decision to compromise even before he spoke. "Have dinner with me tonight. I'll come to your hotel. What time suits you?"

He knew her hotel.

The hunter, Leigh thought again.

But he couldn't take away her right to choose.

There was so much to think about...and still to do. The memory of why she'd come to the funeral sliced through the muddle in her mind. She'd wanted a sense of family again. It probably suited Richard to discount any relationship she might have with her mother and sisters, but Leigh couldn't dismiss them so easily. She'd come here today to be with them, not him, and regardless of all he'd said, she still wanted to know if she meant anything to the people who had shared most of her life.

"You did want this with me, Leigh," he said, his eyes focused intently on her expression.

"And I don't regret it," she assured him, forcing a smile to release him from any concern over recriminations on her part. Nevertheless, marriage was an entirely different question and she was not about to be pushed on it either way. She needed to know more of Richard Seymour, more than the glimpses she'd seen this afternoon. "Dinner tonight is fine," she decided. "Make it eight o'clock."

"Good!" Relief and pleasure in his eyes.

"I'll see you then," she pressed, slowly and rather tentatively swinging her legs off the cane sofa and sitting up to encourage his departure.

He shot her a quick scrutiny, then nodded as though assuring himself there was no mistake about her intentions. "We are right together, Leigh," he stated decisively. "Don't let anything your mother or sisters say distort that truth."

She didn't agree or disagree, not wanting to prolong this encounter with him, but as she watched him leave, the thought ran through her mind that everyone held a different truth within themselves, and finding it could be difficult, let alone expressing it.

She wasn't sure of Richard's truth.

She wasn't sure of her own…at least not where he was concerned.

One thing she was sure of…having been hit by a shattering range of different perceptions this afternoon, Leigh wasn't about to make hasty judgements about her family. Perhaps as a teenager she'd been too self-absorbed to see or comprehend the pressures on their lives. It was impossible to know what really went on inside other people unless they showed it. She'd never had the faintest idea that Richard had no birthright to the Seymour name.

He closed the door behind him, making the summerhouse dark again, dark and private. Light did filter down from the sky dome at the central peak of the roof, enough to see by, though the grey day made it dim.

Leigh looked around her, recognising all the furniture,

a little surprised it hadn't been changed. Though hardly anyone used this place, she reminded herself, recalling how it had provided a handy escape for her when tensions were running high, a private bolt-hole where she could count on not being disturbed.

A perfect place for secret intimacy, Leigh thought, smiling ironically over its handiness to Richard at the critical moment. Then the thought struck her with heart-stopping force.

Was this where *she* had been conceived...her mother with the Italian gardener?

Her hands instantly flew to her stomach. No...her mind screamed. Frantically, she numbered the days since her last period. Seven. Only seven. She was surely safe from pregnancy. The time of fertility would have to be further on from this. Relief rolled through her. If Richard was counting on a baby to turn her into his bride, he was in for disappointment.

Though he couldn't have calculated on impregnating her, could he? Not beforehand. He hadn't used protection, but going through with this intimacy hadn't been his decision, and he couldn't have known she wasn't using something. Until he'd realised she was a virgin. He had hesitated then...so definitely no premeditation.

Another roll of relief...followed by a strong wave of resolution.

She was not going to repeat her mother's life, having baby after baby in pursuit of the desired son. The sex of a child should never mean that much and no way would Leigh let it mean what Lawrence Durant had made of it. A child should be loved for its own sake.

Was there any love for her...just a scrap of it somewhere? She needed to spend time with her mother and sisters. Surely now with Lawrence gone, the real truth could emerge, without any fear of a backlash.

Then tonight…

Yes, she wanted to be with Richard tonight. She wanted…needed…him to show her more of himself…to make what had happened between them this afternoon more right.

If that was possible.

CHAPTER FIVE

THE Durant mansion finally emptied of guests...except for Richard Seymour. To Leigh's frustration, her mother hung onto him, insisting he stay and have coffee with the family. Her sisters were clustered around him like an entourage, eagerly adding their pressure to the invitation. Which he accepted, plunging Leigh into a torment of doubt about his intentions.

His words to her in the summer-house came flooding back... *We are right together. Don't let anything your mother and sisters say distort that truth.*

Was he deliberately staying on to protect what gains he thought he'd made with her? She had evaded being near him since she'd returned to the house, needing to regain her composure before facing her family in the privacy she'd been longing for. And now he was depriving her of it!

Wasn't her promise to meet him tonight enough, she thought in a burst of angry resentment. Or was he playing more than one hand, careful not to offend her other sisters in case one of them had to be his second choice? After all, he had no guarantee she *would* consent to his plans.

Leigh tried to set her turmoil aside as she trailed behind the others, heading for the more intimate lounge room. Whatever his purpose, Richard couldn't stay indefinitely. She simply had to wait out more time.

She wished one of her sisters would fall back and

hang onto her arm, or simply say something to her, at least give some hint of how they felt about her turning up again. The sense of aloneness was somehow worse now than when she had lived here. Was she being deliberately ostracised or was it up to her to take some initiative?

Leigh fought past a host of inhibitions and quickened her pace to catch Nadine, who at twenty-six was closest to her in age. "Can we have a talk, Nadine?" she asked, touching her arm in appeal.

"Not now, Leigh." She wrinkled her nose and tossed her artfully streaked and tousled blonde mane. "Bad taste, isn't it, turning up today?"

Leigh was rattled by the accusation. "I didn't think anyone would mind."

This earned a scathing look. "Playing Cinderella in public. Where on earth did you get that suit? In a bargain basement?"

Her clothes offended? But Richard had said she looked good. Was it really so obvious they were relatively inexpensive? Leigh could feel her cheeks burning. She hadn't meant to play Cinderella. Though compared to Nadine, who was poured into a soft black leather suit with calf-length boots to match, she probably did look…*cheap*.

"Now see what you've done, holding me back?" Nadine hissed at her as they entered the lounge room. "Felicity has snaffled Richard."

Her very elegant oldest sister was drawing him into sharing a sofa with her.

"Why don't you just disappear again, Leigh? No one wants you here."

Stunned by Nadine's hostility, Leigh hesitated. Her

sister flounced forward and commandeered the coffee service which had already been set out. She was full of sweet smiles for Richard, asking him what he'd like.

"Don't just hang there, Leigh," her mother reproved. "Come and sit down."

She indicated the armchair which was fairly close to the one she had chosen at the other end of the room. Leigh felt a surge of relief. At least her mother was prepared to welcome her company, now that her hostess role was virtually over.

As she skirted the sofas which her other sisters had claimed, she reminded herself Nadine had always considered her a nuisance, especially when she'd been asked to "look after her little sister." With both of them being adults now, she had thought it might be different. However, it seemed Nadine still harboured a nasty streak, especially when her self-interests were crossed.

Leigh sat down and offered a grateful smile to her mother but Alicia was no longer looking at her. She was keenly observing the scene with her other daughters and Richard. Leigh was left with the uncomfortable impression that she had been neatly removed from it, being placed in this particular armchair. Minutes passed, and her mother didn't so much as glance at her. This further evidence of being ignored was deeply deflating. Nevertheless, she resolved to wait it out.

Nadine brought her mother a cup of coffee, wiggling her derriere as she walked and bending over so far her short skirt rode up to give a provocative view. Except Richard wasn't watching, which gave Leigh some ironic amusement. His attention was focused on Felicity who had one arm hooked along the backrest of the sofa so she could idly brush his shoulder with her fingertips as she engaged him in conversation.

Felicity, the first-born, had always been ''The Princess.'' She had a porcelain beauty; smooth, pale, almost translucent skin, china blue eyes, flawless features and ash-blonde hair, wound into a gleaming French roll today. Tall, with long graceful legs, she wore a superb coat-dress in fine wool crêpe, with satin collar and cuffs. To the teenage Leigh, Felicity had been the perfect model of the unattainable. She was still perfect at thirty.

Leigh's gaze drifted to Vanessa who was now twenty-nine. She had kicked her shoes off and was languorously sprawled on the chaise-longue, her more curvy figure displayed in black lace. Her hair was more a wheat colour, shoulder-length, and a glorious mass of waves and curls. Her eyes were blue-grey and heavy lidded, giving her a slumbrous sexy look, and her full-lipped mouth was pouting in displeasure at being pushed to one side by her more polished sister.

Both Felicity and Vanessa had married wealthy men while Leigh had been living here. She'd been ruled out as a bridesmaid at their weddings. Black hair would look wrong in the photographs. Not that the photographs were on show any more. Neither were their husbands. Divorced, her mother had curtly explained when Leigh had remarked on their absence at the funeral.

Caroline had grabbed the end seat of the sofa adjacent to where Richard sat. Her yellow-blonde hair was styled into a sleek, ear-level bob and she looked very sophisticated in a black velvet suit. She had a coltish figure and her features were thinner than her sisters', sharper. She had a sharp tongue, as well, Leigh remembered. Did that account for her not being married at twenty-seven?

Nadine sat down next to Caroline, having overlooked Leigh in her coffee serving. So there they were, all four of her sisters, all available to Richard and bent on attracting his attention. Did they want him or did they *need* him? Leigh wondered, struggling to suppress the needs he'd stirred in herself.

Being ignorant of the full contents of Lawrence's will, she had no idea what had been settled on his wife and daughters. Lawrence might have been mean enough to attach provisional clauses to their bequests, pulling financial strings since he could no longer manipulate personal ones. If this was so, she was far better off out of it and not tied to anything. At least she felt free to arrange her own future as she liked.

The Cinderella tag wormed its way into her mind again. Her black suit had been on a bargain rack in a Perth department store, and certainly didn't feature a designer label. Her plain court shoes were not Italian, unlike her real father, she thought with secret irony. She was now used to living on a budget. Her sisters weren't.

Her home life and her companions at the exclusive private school she'd gone to in her teen years had given her a force-fed education on desirable labels. Even though she'd been out of that one-upmanship game for some years, Leigh could still identify the distinctive styles.

Her mother, Alicia, was definitely wearing a Chanel suit, very smart and subdued. Felicity's coat-dress was undoubtedly a Carla Zampatti creation. Vanessa's lace had to be a Collette Dinnigan design. Caroline's velvet was unmistakably Trent Nathan. The leather Nadine favoured was probably from Saba.

Leigh knew she was looking at thousands of dollars

before even beginning to assess the cost of shoes, hats and handbags. Not that it mattered to her. It was simply indicative of a very wealthy life-style which all of them probably wished to maintain. Image, she knew, was important in the lives they led.

Richard could certainly keep them in the manner to which they were accustomed. Yet for all their efforts to snatch and hold his attention, as far as Leigh could see, he was totally impartial in his manner to them; polite, attentive, yet very self-contained. Was he keeping his choices open, Leigh wondered, finding herself hating the thought.

She wanted to be *special* to him.

Yet why should she be?

The question of why he'd asked her first began to nag her. Was he bored with her sisters, having known them longer? Did he see her as the easiest one to manage? Was he simply swayed by sexual chemistry? She squirmed a little, remembering the highly volatile nature of their coming together in the summer-house.

Wanting...was that the key element?

She tried to look at him objectively, needing to work out what was really driving him. As though sensing her scrutiny, he shot her a quick, enigmatic look, then deliberately set his coffee cup and saucer down and rose to his feet, targeting her mother with an appreciative smile.

"Thank you for your hospitality..."

"You're welcome to stay to dinner, Richard," Alicia swiftly interposed.

"It's very kind of you, but I'd rather take my leave now," he replied firmly.

Felicity leapt to her feet. "Time for me to go, too. I'll accompany you out, Richard."

He frowned at her, then pointedly transferred his gaze to Leigh. "Aren't you forgetting you haven't seen your sister for six years?"

Leigh's heart squeezed tight. She didn't want him to order what wasn't worth anything unless it was freely given. Though in the next instant she realised even *his* opinion on her behalf was not going to count.

"Oh, Leigh..." Felicity trilled a dismissive laugh. "What on earth would we have to talk about after all these years apart?" Her eyes flicked to the black sheep, chilling in their disinterest. "We never did have anything in common, did we, sweetie?"

The awful condescension kept Leigh silent.

"That may be different now, Felicity," Richard said in a silkily dangerous tone. "Why don't you stay and find out?"

Leigh clenched her hands. Of all the times she'd wanted him to be her champion, he chose now, when it was totally inappropriate. Or was he deliberately underlining the emptiness he knew was here, making her know it, too?

"What for?" Felicity argued, shrugging off the suggestion. "Leigh will probably be gone again tomorrow."

Vanessa sinuously unfolded herself from the chaise-longue and hooked her arm around Richard's, batting her eyelashes at him flirtatiously. "Why not come back to my place for dinner, Richard? I'm sure Leigh only wants to talk to Mummy."

He shot a hard, purposeful look at Leigh. "Thank you, but I have other plans, Vanessa." He gave a general nod around the company as he extricated his arm. "Please excuse me, all of you."

Her sisters watched his departure with grim-faced displeasure. None of them had made the impression they'd wanted to make on him and he was removing the opportunity to further their own ends.

It suddenly struck Leigh that Richard had stayed to keep them all together. For *her*. Just as he was leaving them all here. For *her*. Giving her what she'd wanted. As he'd promised. Her heart fluttered wildly at this evidence of his caring. Or was it another calculated move, showing her that what she'd wanted from her family was not here for her? That was already miserably obvious.

The moment the door was closed behind him, Caroline swung her head around to glare at her mother. "Honestly, Mum, couldn't you have fobbed Leigh off to some other time?" she demanded critically. "Richard has always had a soft spot for her."

A soft spot? Was there some heart as well as purpose in his proposal?

"So how do you think it would look to him if I'd done that, Caroline?" Alicia retorted wearily.

Leigh's heart twisted with even more misery. Politics. No caring for her at all.

"What do you mean...a soft spot?" Felicity snapped, looking incredulously at Leigh.

Caroline snorted derisively. "If you weren't so damned full of yourself, you would have noticed how Richard always took the heat off Leigh whenever Dad had a go at her in front of him. Usually he asked you a question, which you probably found flattering, but he was really protecting our poor little done by sister."

That much was true. Leigh recognised it now.

Felicity's chin lifted haughtily. "Richard *was* interested in me. He's always been interested in me."

"Oh, don't put on your airs and graces with us," Vanessa sniped. "He was nothing but polite to you. No sparks at all." She targeted Leigh with a mean, narrow-eyed look. "And just why have you been hovering around all day, like a black crow waiting to pounce? What's your game, Leigh?"

"A slice of the estate if she can get it," Nadine slid in sneeringly. "Look at her! Probably raided a charity shop for those clothes."

"She's got no chance of breaking the will," Caroline declared, pushing herself up from the sofa. Again she addressed Alicia sharply, "Might be worthwhile paying her to get out of here, Mum. She could spoil our pitch."

"Don't be ridiculous, Caroline!" Vanessa jeered.

"Didn't manage to vamp Richard into going to your place, did you?" Caroline whipped back. "Ask yourself why, Vanessa." She pointed at Leigh. "He was considering her!"

All four sisters turned to glare at her.

Felicity looking down her nose... "You really don't belong here, Leigh."

Nadine spiteful... "You were disinherited."

Vanessa mocking... "I can't believe you're a threat, but I'd prefer not to have a distraction. The sooner you disappear again, the better."

Caroline ruthless... "We don't need you. Just get out, Leigh, and stay out."

Having delivered that judgement Caroline stalked out of the room, followed by the others in quick succession. Leigh watched them go, too sickened to raise any protest. In a way, she supposed she had thwarted their desires to snag Richard's attention and hold it, but no reasoning in the world could ease the pain of their cold and callous rejection of her return to their midst.

She wasn't wanted.

No one cared about her.

No one was the least bit interested in her.

The cuckoo had flown away and they had probably all thought *good riddance*.

Into the silence of devastated hopes came her mother's voice, tired and frayed. "What do you want, Leigh?"

Leigh was still looking at the door Felicity had shut so decisively behind all four of her sisters. Half-sisters, she reminded herself, though there was no consolation in that brutal fact. It took a concerted effort to look at her mother, who had probably only stayed to find out if her unwanted fifth daughter meant to cause trouble.

Alicia's face was taut, her eyes biting in their disapproval. A leaden weight descended on Leigh's wounded heart. It was more of the same, even with Lawrence dead. There was no place for her here. Never would be. The pattern had been set long ago and no one saw any reason for it to change.

"What do you think I want, Mother?" she dragged out, mocking herself more than the woman who'd given birth to her.

"Why don't you tell me?" came the wary reply—a reply that gave nothing away—a reply that put a cold, impersonal distance between them.

Leigh couldn't bear to keep looking at her. She knew, beyond a shadow of a doubt, her mother was expecting her to ask for a share in Lawrence's estate. Her gaze wandered idly around the room—a blue and white room that had no warmth in it, just furnishings and pieces of art that cost a lot of money, flagrant exhibitions of buying power for others to admire and envy. There was no heart in it, no heart anywhere in this ostentatious mansion.

"Did you think of me at all in the past six years, Mother?" she asked, wanting to know if she had been missed, if only a tiny bit.

"Naturally, I thought of you," came the too smooth answer. "I hoped you were happy in your choice to make a life for yourself."

While she dissociated herself from it, Leigh thought, probably relieved to have "her mistake" removed so it wasn't a constant thorn in her side.

"Did you worry about me?"

A slight pause, then a slowly chosen reply. "I respected your choice, Leigh. I felt sure you'd contact us if you were in need."

Which required no action on Alicia's part, none at all. Not that Leigh had expected any *worry* over her disappearance at the time. Remembering back, she realised the truth of her position in the Durant family had been laid bare then. It was time and distance that had raised hopes for something else, a different interpretation of actions and non-actions.

"Did you wonder how I survived, kept myself going without your help?" she asked, determined on being absolutely fair before making a final judgement.

"Well, you obviously did or you wouldn't be here now."

The dry intonation goaded Leigh into looking her mother in the face again. "You don't care, do you?" she accused flatly. "You have no interest whatsoever in what I've done, where I've been, how I managed."

An impatient grimace. "You always had the option of coming home, Leigh. No one banished you."

Home to the kind of mental and emotional abuse her mother had never tried to stop? Leigh had wanted to believe the neglect and indifference was defensive, done out of fear of drawing Lawrence's wrath. But she couldn't believe that now.

"I was eighteen, Mother," Leigh reminded her. "In shock. Disinherited because you admitted to having me by another man."

No comment.

The silence heightened the memory of that dreadful night, the hate-filled revelations that had poured over her head because she had dared to stand up for herself and appeal to both of them for a fairer deal...her mother screaming, "You drove me to it, Lawrence, with your constant harping on a son."...Lawrence jeering, "And you thought a cuckoo would do?"

On and on it had gone...the contempt, the recriminations, the wounding, neither of them caring what she felt...the object of their personal battle...the object who was mangled between them as they tore into each other...the object of failed ambitions, thus being forever offensive to them.

Yes, she had understood it then.

Yet still she searched her mother's face for some hint of conscience about her. "When you discovered I was gone, did you think I was in a fit state to make my own way?"

Alicia's eyes hardened. "It was *your* choice. I had my own battles to fight at the time."

"So you didn't worry about me. I was—let us say— one less problem to deal with."

"You were always a problem, Leigh," was the terse reply.

"Much easier to be rid of me."

"Don't put words into my mouth," Alicia snapped.

Leigh couldn't let it go. "I don't suppose you reported me to the police as a missing person," she pressed.

"Don't be absurd! Lawrence would never have allowed it.'

"Perhaps you hired a private investigator to check that I was not in any trouble."

As Richard had...Richard declaring he'd done it because he'd cared...the only one who cared...

Alicia sighed, impatient with the inquisition. "I expected a call from you if you were in trouble." Her tone was loaded with exasperation.

"What if I was in no position to call, Mother? Did you worry about that?"

"Oh, for God's sake, Leigh! What are you going on about? You're here, aren't you? Safe and sound?"

No thanks to you or any member of my family, Leigh thought bitterly. Her gaze ran derisively over the Chanel suit. "I was just thinking that what you spent on the mourning outfit you have on today would have paid a private investigator to keep tabs on me for a while...if you'd cared enough to worry about me."

Alicia instantly leaned forward, pouncing on what she understood better than anything else. "Right! So you think you're owed a chunk of money and that's why you've come, now that you don't have to face Lawrence for it."

For several moments, Leigh's revulsion was so strong she couldn't speak. Her stomach churned violently. Her mind exploded under the sheer weight of all the burdens it had carried and whirled into the darkness of a world without love, the darkness of deep and abiding injustice. She wasn't aware of forming the words that spat out of that darkness. They came of their own accord, pieces of emotional chaos that had been gathering inside her all day long.

"Wrong, Mother! You can't pay me off...as you did my real father. And I won't disappear for you."

The eager satisfaction was wiped out. All colour drained from Alicia's face. "What do you know of that? Why do you bring it up?"

Ah, the triumph of doing some shattering herself! The darkness gained ground from it. Her voice instinctively copied Richard's silky dangerous tone. "Oh, that's just between you and me, Mother. We keep scandals buried in this family, don't we?"

Alicia sat back, adopting a pose of impervious hauteur. "Are you threatening me, Leigh?"

Suddenly it was easy to laugh. The madness of her hopes was really funny. Here she was, being seen as a threat and she'd come as a beggar for affection. "Not at all," she spluttered in wild amusement. "I came here today to find out where I stood with you. And with my sisters. Now I know."

Her mother looked totally bamboozled.

Leigh smiled at her as she stood up to take her leave. "Goodbye, Mother. I find I don't want to have anything more to do with you. Or your other daughters."

She started towards the door. Her legs were shaky. She willed strength into them.

"Where are you going, Leigh?" Hard suspicion in the question shot after her. No belief at all in the last farewell.

"To my hotel," Leigh answered, enjoying the light carelessness in her voice. It was good to show she could match the non-caring she had met.

"What do you intend to do?"

The answer came to Leigh, the beautiful perfect answer, pushing out of the darkness and shining with the glorious purity of justice. She stopped and half-turned, wanting to beam it straight at the mother who had always put ambition first. Alicia should really appreciate this. It was, after all, the ambition she held dearest at the moment.

"I intend to marry Richard Seymour."

The shock this decisive declaration raised was deeply satisfying.

"What?" Alicia croaked incredulously.

Leigh smiled. "He chose me, Mother. Not Felicity, not Vanessa, not Caroline, not Nadine...me. And I shall marry him as soon as it can be arranged."

On that triumphant note she left, shutting the door on the Durant mansion and everyone in it.

CHAPTER SIX

THE hours between throwing down the gauntlet to her mother and the eight o'clock deadline with Richard Seymour churned past for Leigh. From time to time the voice of sanity tried to drag her back from the brink...

You don't need this. You've made a good, normal, stable life for yourself in Broome. You can walk away, put it all at a distance again and never look back.

But overwhelming that voice in fierce, rebellious waves came a deep, soul-driven cry for justice...

All these years...the loser, the rejected one, the despised one, the one worth nothing. Why shouldn't she be the winner for once? Why shouldn't she take the prize? She'd always wanted Richard to be her champion. Let him be that now, openly, unmistakably, not just having a soft spot for her, but standing beside her, fighting anyone who cast any slur on her. *Her husband!*

The time has come for us, he'd said. So what if that was linked to dancing on Lawrence Durant's grave together! The kind of pact he'd offered her was grounded in sharing a common background. Who else would ever know her as he did, understanding the loneliness, the sense of separation from people who'd led more normal lives?

The plain truth was she'd been living a fiction of normality in Broome, a veneer of stability. Her darkest inner truths lay here, probably bound up more with Richard Seymour than anyone else. But she couldn't let him know that because he'd use it to get what he wanted. A hunter used everything to get what he wanted and she had no illusions about that side of Richard Seymour.

Ambition came first with him. It would be foolish to fantasise any really special feeling for her. Even though Richard had shown more caring towards her than anyone else, it had always been caring at a safe distance. He'd been very discreet about *being her friend*, and Leigh had no doubt he'd been even more discreet about keeping tabs on her, ensuring no harm came to him from his *caring*.

All the same, *she* was his first choice in the marriage stakes. Which had to mean something positive towards her, more positive than anything he felt for her sisters. Leigh comforted herself with that thought even as she realised she mustn't make too much of it.

She had to keep her mind straight on this. In agreeing to marry him, she didn't have to give him her head on a plate. No-one was ever going to take absolute control over her life. She wouldn't submit to another Lawrence Durant. Richard had better understand that. She had terms, as well, terms he had to respect if they were to share a future together.

What she needed was a plan of action...something firm she could hang onto...something that would show Richard she was purposeful, too, not just a pawn in his game to be manipulated as he willed. A wife was more than that. The need to be more than that to him welled up in her and wouldn't let go.

Somehow she managed to harness her erratic thoughts long enough to work out what kind of understanding she required from him in this marriage. She had priorities, too, and getting control of a financial empire wasn't one of them. She wouldn't be forced into having baby after baby after baby, just to get a son. And if Richard started abusing her rights as a person in any way, nothing would keep her with him. She wouldn't allow him to hurt her like that.

Despite this fierce bout of reasoning, when his knock came at precisely eight o'clock, Leigh was swamped by a sense of panic. It took all her will-power to get a grip on herself, to open the door. She stood back a little, just looking at him...this man she'd decided to marry.

He hadn't worn a suit, though the clothes he'd chosen could probably go anywhere; royal blue skivvy, grey leather jacket, grey slacks. The casual look didn't change anything. He still emitted the same charismatic power of knowing what he wanted and having the unshakeable will to pull out all stops to get it. She felt her skin start to burn as his laser blue eyes raked her appearance, assessing what it meant, how he could use it.

She hadn't dressed for dinner. She had no intention of dining with him, nor even talking with him beyond establishing what was to be done. She was afraid that any further intimacy with him at this point could weaken her decisions. Better to avoid it.

Her hair was still wound up and pinned into a rather messy topknot from the long hot shower she'd taken, and the oyster-pink satin wraparound covered a slip-nightie in the same colour. She was ready for bed, but not with him.

"I don't want dinner, Richard, and I don't want sex," she fired at him point-blank, forcefully defensive in struggling to deny the panic. "There are a few things to be arranged between us and that's it," she went on, amazing herself with the firm tone of her voice. "You can come in on that understanding."

He nodded, shrewd enough not to make any comment as he stepped into her room. Leigh shut the door and stayed by it, ready to let him out again the moment she was finished with him. Despite the resolution—the plan—seething through her mind, his actual physical presence stirred a host of vulnerabilities she didn't want to feel, didn't want to examine, either. This meeting had to be about promises, made and kept.

"Have you had any second thoughts about choosing me to marry?" she demanded, wary of making a fool of herself.

His gaze was fixed on her travelling bag which lay on the bed, unzipped, the suit she'd worn today folded neatly on top of the rest of her things which she hadn't bothered unpacking. He swung around slowly, noting the jeans, T-shirt, windcheater and underclothes she'd set on a chair, ready to don in the morning. The hotel room was very basic, which was all Leigh could afford. Richard missed nothing in it, clearly assessing the situation before facing her.

"I want *you*, Leigh. No-one else," he answered simply, his eyes searing hers with a blaze of desire that set every nerve end in Leigh's body twitching.

Her stomach contracted, her toes curled, her heart shot bolts of heat through her bloodstream, and her mind momentarily lost its focus. The sheer impact of that look pressed her back against the door, as though she was his prey, feeling cornered. Her hand clutched the doorknob, instinctively seeking a defensive weapon.

"Don't you take one step towards me, Richard!" she cried, wildly challenging his intent, despite her decision to take him as her husband. She was *not* going to be a victim in his scheme. Nor would she be seduced to his will.

He remained where he was. "You have the floor," he said, gesturing an open invitation that reduced any sense of threat, yet still there was a simmer in his eyes that let her know the desire was temporarily harnessed but very much alive and kicking.

At least they had that going for them, Leigh recklessly reasoned. What they'd done—felt—in the summerhouse wasn't a one-off thing. It could happen again now if she let it, but it wouldn't resolve what she needed resolved.

"I'll marry you, but I have conditions," she blurted out.

The tensile spring in his body eased. "State them," he said equably.

"*You* make all the arrangements."

His eyes narrowed slightly. "You don't want to plan a wedding?"

Without a mother or a father or anyone who would be interested in her being a bride? How could he even imagine it? For a moment, Leigh's mind went totally blank. The idea of a *wedding* hadn't occurred to her, only the fact of a marriage between them. If he wanted *a wedding*...no, she would have to stay here for that to be managed and she recoiled from being anywhere within reach of her mother and sisters until this marriage became fact.

"Plan whatever suits you. I don't care," she declared, turbulently rejecting any wish for a public celebration.

She had no-one to share it with, and that bare truth only emphasised the lack of any real connections. Even her friends in Broome were more congenial acquaintances, sharing interests but nothing deeper than that. She couldn't imagine any of them going to the expense of flying across the continent to her wedding. They'd wish her well and let her go, maybe remembering her occasionally.

"Just leave me out of it until our wedding day, Richard," she said decisively.

Then she would have *him*, for better or for worse! *He* hadn't let her go. All these years watching over her...suddenly Leigh felt good about that. She wasn't *nothing* to Richard.

"So your family is not to be involved?" he said, watching her keenly.

Her chin went up in defiant pride. "I don't consider I have a family any more."

No comment. In his eyes was the knowledge of what she'd been through with her mother and sisters this afternoon, not sympathetic knowledge, more an assessment of how deeply it had affected her, and Leigh hated his understanding of her stance.

It was shaming, painful, yet in this awful, intimate sharing of emptiness and darkness, there was also a strange consoling that no-one else could give. He *knew*. He knew precisely where she was coming from...the injustices she had suffered, the rejections, the wiping off as of no account to anybody.

It provided a kind of kinship she doubted she'd find with any other man. Whether that was a good or bad kinship, she didn't know. What it did was take the edge off the sense of aloneness she'd felt all her life.

"You don't have any preference regarding how we get married?" he asked quietly.

Her mouth twitched into a mocking little smile. "It does need to be legal." His proposal was based on legalities so he should appreciate that point.

"It will certainly be legal," he assured her, his own mouth quirking, yet there was a flash of something dark and dangerous in his eyes as though she'd struck a core of secret purpose, beyond anything anyone knew about him.

A convulsive little shiver ran down her spine but she resolutely ignored it. Everyone had a secret self. As long as they respected each other, this marriage probably had as much a chance of working as any other.

"I'm booked on flights back to Broome tomorrow," she announced. "I'm not staying here, Richard. I have business to see to if I'm to shift my life to Sydney. I presume you can see to whatever documentation is required."

He nodded. "I trust you will be back for the wedding."

"The day before," she promised.

"And you intend to be my wife, living with me?" His eyes probed hers with merciless intent.

"Yes, but I don't intend to be a baby machine for you," she stated fiercely. Never, in a million years would she repeat what her mother had done. Not for anything or anyone.

"At least one child, Leigh," Richard barrelled straight back at her.

She took a deep breath and determinedly challenged him. "If we have a daughter first and you respond badly, I'll leave you."

A glimmer of very strong feeling flashed into his eyes. "Any child of mine will be precious to me."

There was a strong edge to his voice, too, instantly recalling to Leigh the circumstances of his birth... another cuckoo, perhaps shunted to one side because he didn't belong as he should. Or was she grasping at straws, needing to feel reassured that her decision to marry him would not lead to an intolerable situation?

"Having a daughter instead of a son will prolong the time you don't have full control of the company," she reminded him.

"I don't intend to stand still in anticipation of the terms of Lawrence's will being fulfilled, Leigh. Others might...I won't. The Durant company will be mine, one way or another."

Ruthless purpose suddenly emanated from him, and Leigh was forcefully struck with the realisation there was nothing soft about this man. He was hard, through and through, committed to a course nothing was going to stop. A very dangerous man.

Had Lawrence Durant recognised that or had Richard hid his hand from his mentor? Leigh suspected the latter. His choice to marry her was a blatant flouting of Lawrence's will. A victory over Lawrence, he'd called it this afternoon. What other victories did Richard have planned?

"So marrying me is only a ploy in whatever game you're about," she put to him, keenly watching his expression.

His eyes crinkled in amusement. "More than a ploy, Leigh. A step that needs to be taken. It also pleases me to marry you."

Pleasure curled her stomach. It was a struggle to keep questioning him. "Personal, as well as business?"

He smiled his heart-mashing smile. "On many levels, very personal."

Even as everything inside her squirmed and pulsed with treacherous excitement, Leigh fiercely told herself it would be stupid to let herself become too vulnerable to that smile. There would always be a part of Richard Seymour he'd keep to himself—the part Lawrence Durant had found so admirable—and she didn't really want to know that part.

So long as he let her be the person she was, they could coexist, couldn't they, sharing what they did share? She needed to feel a *kinship*, to have some sense of belonging to a kind of continuance instead of a blank nothing.

Still smiling, his eyes caressing her with a warmth that threatened to melt her will-power, he said, "Your passion always appealed to me."

"Passion?" Leigh queried, trying to fit the word to the teenager he'd known.

"You radiate intensity, Leigh. Always have. And I hope, always will." His smile tilted musingly. "Maybe from your Italian heritage."

It was a new thought. Leigh instantly wondered how much she took after her real father. Apart from temperament, which she supposed could be passed on genetically, there was the creative side of her nature. Gardeners could be creative. She thought of her pottery enterprise in Broome, which wasn't exactly lucrative, but she loved working with clay...the shapes and colours, the tactile pleasure of it.

"Any more conditions?" Richard prompted.

"Yes. One more. I want to go on with my pottery. You must know about that from your surveillance on me."

He nodded. "Once you're my wife, we'll choose a property that suits both of our living requirements. You can have a kiln built. Whatever you like, Leigh. I have no objection whatsoever to your pursuing your art during the day…"

He started walking towards her and there was no more giving in his eyes, only an intensity of purpose that encompassed her in a relentless grip. "…but the nights are mine," he said softly. "Understand that, Leigh. The nights are mine."

Leigh could feel herself trembling, whether in fear or anticipation she didn't know. Having screwed her mind to the sticking point of laying down her conditions, she simply hadn't thought of how he saw their life together, beyond the legalities that had forced his hand. Except…his hand wasn't really forced, was it? Hadn't he implied the marriage was more a *sleight of hand* while he pursued his own agenda?

He reached her while she was still in a whirl of confusion. He didn't touch her, but he was so close, she found herself holding her breath and her temples were drumming from her wildly accelerated heartbeat. She couldn't tear her eyes from the glittering intent in his.

"Are we agreed?" he asked softly, and even his voice affected her physically…sexually…

"Yes," she whispered.

"I don't take kindly to being made a fool of, Leigh. From the moment I leave this room, I'll be acting on the word you've given me tonight, on several levels, all of them important to me. Your word is your bond. No second thoughts. Total commitment. Is that understood?"

For a moment the gravity of the phrase—total commitment—shook her resolution. Then she hastily reminded herself Richard had accepted all her conditions. As for sharing his bed every night, once she was his wife, how could that not be acceptable, given the lust they seemed to arouse in each other? She didn't have the experience to know if something so physical lasted for long, but it felt like a positive factor.

"We're agreed," she affirmed with as much strength as she could muster.

He smiled and his eyes suddenly danced with wicked provocation. "Is a kiss to seal our bargain permissible or is the *don't touch* command still in force?"

A kiss…why not? Just to make certain it truly did feel right, a taste of what was to come. Realising she was still clutching the doorknob, Leigh released it and lifted both hands to the broad shoulders she was trusting to carry her decisions through.

With her permission implicit, Richard didn't wait for words. He swept her against him and there was not a trace of seductive intent in his kiss. It was hotly explosive, claiming her mouth in a passionate drive to take all she would give him. It was exhilarating, and deeply, deeply satisfying, feeling his desire pouring into her, knowing it was real and true, feeling her own desire rush to meet it, join with it, exult in the merging.

It was a powerful promise of exciting pleasure to be shared with him and Leigh was left dazed by it when Richard pulled away from her. He touched her lips with his fingertips in a gentle salute…or was it a sealing of his imprint inside her?

"I'll look forward to our wedding night," he murmured, his voice husky with sweet satisfaction, his eyes glowing with an inner vision that centred on her…as his…when there would be no pulling back from taking all he wanted.

He left, taking her consent to their marriage with him. More than her consent, Leigh thought dizzily, her commitment. And she wouldn't go back on it. He might be a dangerous man in many ways but he'd left her with one unassailable conviction. There was no other man for her. Never would be. Richard Seymour owned part of her soul that no one else could.

CHAPTER SEVEN

LEIGH sat on a rock, watching her last sunset at Cable Beach. Or maybe it wasn't her last. Who knew what the future would bring? Tomorrow she would fly to Sydney. The day after she would marry Richard Seymour and start another life, very different from this one, she imagined.

She'd disposed of most of her pottery. All her bills were paid. Everything she wanted to take with her was packed away in storage, ready to be sent on when she had a firm address. Friends had given her a farewell luncheon party today. Her ties to this place were virtually cut now. Only a few clothes and personal toiletries were left to be put in the luggage she would carry tomorrow.

Her gaze drifted down the long stretch of firm sand. All sorts of vehicles—cars, four-wheel drive wagons, small trucks, bikes—were parked along it, facing the water. Music was playing from portable stereos. People had unloaded foldaway deck chairs and picnic tables. Cold drinks and nibbles were being consumed. The mood was one of happy relaxation. It was an evening ritual in Broome, coming to watch the sunset at the end of the day. The news of the world could wait. Here, nature commanded first viewing.

A string of camels carried tourists on a slow amble along the water's edge, their rhythmic, swaying movement almost hypnotic. No hurry. No stress. Just the sight of them injected a calm pleasure. Leigh doubted she would feel any calmness tomorrow, but she was committed to facing whatever came with Richard...facing and dealing with it.

Six weeks it had been since the fateful night of giving him her word. The very next day at the airport terminal in Sydney, she'd been paged to meet a jeweller who had measured her ring finger. People sent by Richard had flown to Broome with papers for her to sign, a prenuptial agreement, documents that were meaningless to her. She wasn't after his money. The jeweller had come, too, bringing her a magnificent solitaire diamond engagement ring which must have cost a fortune. Tomorrow she would put it on.

But tonight...this time was just for herself. She watched the luminous yellow sun changing to red as it started to dip into the ocean. There were no clouds to reflect its colour. The sky was a soft lavender, the water a silvery aquamarine. It was beautiful, peaceful, the freshness of the air making everything feel clean and good, far, far away from any sense of pollution. A simple life this...and she was giving it up for what?

To balance the scales?

To heal what never had been healed?

Or to have Richard Seymour?

All three, she thought, but mostly the last. And where it would lead she didn't know. It was a journey she had to take, for good or ill. Only then would she know. There was no point in thinking about it. Doing it would tell her whether it was worthwhile or not.

The sun slipped to a mere sliver of burning red on the horizon, then was gone. The light changed, colours fading, the final setting of the day. The setting of six years of being alone, Leigh thought, standing up to walk away…walk towards a commitment of living intimately with a man who probably meant more than he should to her, the man bent on taking Lawrence Durant's throne in the financial world.

He was waiting for her.

The flight to Sydney had landed on time, exactly 12: 15 PM, which gave her the afternoon to do some necessary shopping. Leigh reached the top of the escalator leading down to the hall where carousels circulated incoming luggage. She expected someone to meet her. Richard wouldn't leave her wandering around, wondering where to go next. Every move from here on would be meticulously planned to achieve his purpose. Even from afar she'd felt the relentless beat of his will.

But still she wasn't anticipating his presence at the airport terminal. It was like being suddenly hit by a bolt of energy. Her heart skipped a beat. Her gaze was literally tugged to where he stood by a set of exit doors, a mobile telephone held to his ear, but his eyes were fastened on her, eyes that telegraphed such concentrated power, Leigh felt he was claiming her, body and soul.

Her feet must have automatically stepped forward onto the escalator because it was carrying her downwards. Richard tucked the mobile telephone into the breast pocket of his suit as he strode across the hall, clearly aiming to be at the foot of the escalator the moment she stepped off. Momentarily relieved of having to perform any action at all, Leigh watched him as intensely as he watched her.

This was the beginning of their future together. She had been marginally aware of the mantle of leadership he wore on the day of the funeral. Perhaps it had been more muted then, in deference to the public mourning of Lawrence Durant. There was no possible mistaking his air of command now. This man she was about to marry evoked the feeling he could and would take all before him, invincible and...*untouchable*.

Which put Leigh's defences on electric alert.

"Hi!" she said with a controlled little smile as she reached floor level.

"Hi!" he replied, his eyes dancing both amusement at and appreciation of her restrained approach to him. "I'm glad you're safely here."

She nodded. "It's good of you to break your busy schedule to meet me in person."

He laughed, his whole face radiating a delight in her that scrambled her strong sense of caution. He caught her hand and drew her along with him towards the baggage carousels, his eyes still twinkling, putting a ridiculously happy flutter in her heart.

"It would be very remiss of me not to welcome my trump card, Leigh."

Even that remark—centred as it was on his business goals—failed to dampen the rush of treacherous pleasure in being linked to him. The warmth and strength of the hand enfolding hers sent tingles up Leigh's arm. All she could think of was this was the start of not being alone.

"So you still need me," she half-mocked, trying not to show how vulnerable she was to his touch.

"Need and want," he answered, his gaze flicking momentarily to her mouth, lingering long enough to shoot heat through her bloodstream.

Leigh scooped in a quick breath. "I thought it was only the nights you wanted with me," she said drily.

"Ah, that was a minimum requirement. I didn't mean it to be a limitation."

Danger bells rang in her head. She looked sharply at him, acutely aware of his taking power. "What if I don't want more of you?"

He shrugged. "You say so."

"And you'll respect that?"

"Absolutely. I see our marriage as being about mutual agreements, Leigh."

The assurance eased the tightness in her chest. Richard wasn't a tyrant like Lawrence Durant. Not once had he pushed beyond any line she'd drawn. There was no reason not to trust his word.

Noticing he was veering towards the exit doors, she quickly said, "I have luggage to collect, Richard."

"It will be collected and delivered to the hotel. I've booked a suite for you at The Regent. I'll take you there now."

Leigh didn't protest, realising that hanging around at an airport, waiting for luggage to be unloaded, would be a waste of time to Richard. He'd collected *her*. She could probably take such an unnecessary courtesy as a compliment. It certainly indicated a personal note of caring that went beyond calculated profit. That was reassuring, too.

As they emerged from the terminal, a stretch limousine drew into the kerb of the sidewalk, right in line with the exit doors. Richard moved straight to it, opened the back door for her, and in the space of a few moments they were both seated in spacious luxury, behind privacy-tinted windows, and on their way into the city.

"Great timing," Leigh couldn't help commenting.

Richard gave her a quirky smile. "The driver was cruising. I called him in."

The mobile telephone. Of course. Efficiency plus. "Do you ever leave anything to chance, Richard?" she asked curiously.

"One can always be surprised by chance. Your flight could have crashed. The limousine could have been blocked. No one can control everything, Leigh."

"Only as far as it's humanly possible," she teased, sure in her own mind he would plan to cover all foreseeable contingencies.

"Even the human factor can be unpredictable," he answered wryly, reaching across to pick up her left hand, his thumb brushing the ring on her third finger. "I didn't know what you would like. I wondered if you'd prefer a different stone to the traditional diamond."

It amazed her that he'd spent time considering her wishes. She had imagined him simply ordering what he thought appropriate. "You could have asked," she murmured, her voice husky from having to pass a wayward lump of emotion.

The eyes he lifted to hers were very blue, directly challenging. "You were emphatic about being left out of whatever arrangements I wanted to make. It's a bit late to be changing your mind about that, Leigh."

"I'm not. I didn't really care about an engagement ring. If it pleased you to choose this diamond, that's fine by me," she rushed out, feeling weirdly chilled by the sudden emanation of tension from him.

"Then I trust you won't suddenly start caring about the rest of the arrangements I've made."

"I said I'd go along with them and I will."

"Thank you for the reassurance." He smiled his satisfaction, visibly relaxing.

Battle won, Leigh thought. But what battle? She took a deep breath and asked, "What is the plan for tomorrow?"

"The wedding director, Anne Lester, is to meet us at the hotel. She'll take you through everything," he answered matter-of-factly.

Leigh gulped. "A *wedding* director?"

"Not my area of expertise. I hired a specialist."

"You mean we're having a *real* wedding?" Leigh could hear her voice climbing.

He nodded, his eyes glinting with some deep inner relish that had nothing to do with her. "Two hundred guests."

Dear God! He intended to parade their marriage in front of everyone he considered anyone! This was not a private sealing of a personal bargain between them. It was a public flaunting of the Seymour/Durant connection, positively spotlighting it. But for what purpose? Surely it was totally unnecessary.

"Why?" The word shot out, demanding reasons.

His face took on a flintlike hardness and there was not the slightest grain of giving in his eyes. "Because that's the way I want it."

Leigh swallowed hard. There could be no argument about this. She'd given him a free hand. He'd taken it, with a vengeance. "I'll have to buy a wedding dress," she said weakly, shock still thumping through her and panic beginning to shoot out fluttery tentacles.

"I chose one for you."

"You...?" The thought of Richard combing through bridal boutiques boggled her mind.

"I told Anne Lester the style of dress I wanted for you and she presented me with a selection from which I chose," he explained.

"What if it doesn't fit?"

"I believe a fitting is arranged for this afternoon. There'll be time for alterations. The wedding is scheduled for four o'clock tomorrow."

"In a church," Leigh said numbly, mentally crossing off the register office she'd anticipated.

"St. Andrew's Cathedral."

"The reception?"

"The ballroom at The Regent."

All top class! Leigh's mind whirled over the spectacle Richard was determined on. It would probably be the wedding of the year, featuring one of Australia's most eligible bachelors and *the bride of his choice*. In every sense, Leigh wildly added, even to the dress!

"You didn't ask my sisters to be bridesmaids," she fired at him, recoiling from any passive acceptance of that particular "socially correct" appearance.

"No. You will walk alone down the aisle to me."

She heaved a sigh of relief.

"But they did accept their invitations to our wedding, so they will be there as guests," he warned, watching intently for her reaction to this circumstance. "So will your mother."

Inwardly Leigh bridled at the sheer hypocrisy of her family attending a wedding they'd have no desire to celebrate. She really didn't want them there. The vengeful satisfaction she might have felt in their witnessing her marriage to Richard had slipped away from her in the past weeks, her thoughts more on a future with him than scoring off her mother and sisters.

Strangely, she realised they didn't really count any more. In that sense, she supposed it didn't matter if they were there. And there was a certain black irony in their being trapped by their own values into attending a wedding of this social magnitude.

All the same, they were bound to hate it, having to watch her being *the star* while they were relegated to the pews, onlookers, her half-sisters wishing they were *her*, the mother of the bride a mere guest, denied her natural duties, having denied Leigh any *natural* mother love.

In a way, it was justice—an eye for an eye kind of justice. Still, Leigh could have done without them beaming ill will at her while she went through with the ceremony Richard had planned. She looked wonderingly at him. Had he thought this scenario would give her an appropriate measure of much-needed satisfaction for the injustices done to her?

"Why did you invite them?" she asked, wishing she could read his mind.

"Many reasons…"

Foolish to think anything would be simple with Richard. She could sense the complexity of motives tumbling around in his ultra-clever brain as he selected the one he didn't mind her knowing.

"…mostly because I wanted them to see you as I see you."

It surprised her into inquiring, "How *do* you see me, Richard?"

His eyes glittered with the triumph he envisaged. "My bride, my consort, my queen…and homage will be paid to you."

A fierce pride threaded his voice and Leigh wasn't

sure what had dragged it forth, a need to have her shine
for him, or a need to have his power recognised and
acknowledged, even through the wife he'd chosen. Then
he lifted the hand that wore his ring, and pressed a hot,
lingering kiss on her knuckles, his eyes holding hers with
a long simmering blast of raw intent to have and to hold,
and Leigh was thrown into quivering confusion.

Need and want, he'd said to her.

She felt the same—*need and want*—and whatever else
Richard Seymour did, he brought her alive in ways that
made the past six years feel like a long dormant period
where she'd ridden in the shallows, a skimming existence that didn't really experience life at all. She had the
sense of being tugged towards heights and depths, an
inevitable flow birthed in dark underground currents that
swirled through both their lives.

"Should I ask how you see me?" he mused teasingly.

Did it matter to him? Leigh suspected it was quite
irrelevant as long as she fitted into his scheme.
Nevertheless, it would be interesting to have his reaction
to her view.

"The hunter," she said, without preamble or expla-
nation.

It tilted his head and she imagined a multitude of
thoughts racing through it. His expression gave nothing
away. In his eyes was a serious weighing.

"You don't feel trapped, do you, Leigh?"

"No. I know I can walk away if I choose to. There
is no way you can trap me, Richard."

"Then why *the hunter*?"

"I'm not the end goal," she answered simply. "I
don't know what your end goal is but you're hunting it,

and I'd say you've been hunting it for a long, long time.''

"Other people might say I was merely ambitious,'' he blandly remarked.

There was more than ambition behind his ambition, Leigh thought. She'd seen it in his eyes several times, though she couldn't say what it was exactly, only an impression of a dark burning passion that knew no limits in its drive for satisfaction.

She shrugged. "You asked me how I see you.''

"So I did. And your reply was...unpredictable.'' He eyed her with keen interest. "I wonder how many surprises you have for me, Leigh.''

"Perhaps enough to stop you from taking our marriage for granted,'' she tossed back at him, feeling a thrill of exhilaration in having dealt a card he wasn't expecting from her.

He laughed and kissed her hand again, more lightly this time, his eyes flirting. "A wife to be reckoned with. A fascinating prospect.''

He was playing games to cover the truth chord she'd hit. Leigh felt almost dizzy with a strange exultation. He wasn't *untouchable*. Maybe, within the intimacy of their marriage, she would come to understand him as well as he understood her. A fascinating prospect, indeed.

The limousine turned out of the stream of traffic, alerting them both to its arrival at the private driveway up to the hotel entrance. Leigh was glad she had worn her good black slacks and the matching tunic top. The hand-painted scarf she'd fastened around her neck added a bit of distinction. The rock on her finger added more, she assured herself. Entering this hotel as Richard Seymour's fiancée suddenly seemed rather daunting, especially with a wedding director about to steer her through whatever was planned.

The limousine came to a halt. A doorman sprang forward to open the door. Richard alighted and stood by to help her out. The doorman greeted both of them by name and ushered them into the foyer, pointing out where Miss Lester sat, waiting for them.

A very svelte blonde in a smart red suit rose from one of the armchairs grouped in the centre of the foyer. She came forward, smiling, determined to please Richard Seymour, regardless of what she thought of the woman he'd chosen to marry. Leigh estimated her age as late thirties as she came closer, a woman of style and experience.

Richard smoothly performed introductions. "Leigh, this is Anne Lester. Anne, my fiancée, Leigh Durant."

"I'm delighted you're here at last," Anne poured out, offering her hand as her warm brown eyes generated appeal. "I just hope I've got everything right for you."

Leigh pressed her hand lightly and poured back assurance. "I'm sure you've done a superb job. I'm grateful to have it all taken care of."

"It has been a rather unusual assignment, without any input from the bride," Anne commented with a gleam of curiosity.

"Oh, I'm sure the groom's input made up for it," Leigh replied, smiling at Richard to show there was no disagreement.

He curved an arm around her shoulders, hugging her lightly as he smiled back. "I'll leave you in Anne's hands now. I'll call you tonight. Okay?"

"Yes."

Again his gaze dropped to her mouth and she knew

he was tempted to kiss her but he didn't. "Tomorrow," he murmured, and left her with that breath of promise.

She watched him stride back across the foyer to the doorman who stood ready to facilitate his exit. Richard commanded attention as naturally as he breathed. She wondered what kind of boyhood he'd had, and what would be in his heart tomorrow as he stood at the end of the aisle, watching her walk to him, the woman he'd decided to take as his wife.

"You've certainly got yourself a man there, Miss Durant," Anne Lester said admiringly.

Leigh swung her gaze back to the wedding director. An ironic smile tugged at her mouth. "I didn't get him. All this is his idea. I simply said yes."

"But you surely want him." It was said impulsively, out of puzzlement, and almost instantly discretion took over. "I do beg your pardon. I didn't mean to get personal."

Leigh couldn't help laughing. It really was an absurd situation...the prince and the ugly duckling. Nevertheless, it was obvious she needn't feel intimidated by Anne Lester or anyone else in this hotel. The label of Richard Seymour's fiancée lent her automatic respect.

"Well, let's get on with the process of turning me into a swan for him," she said, suddenly feeling quite light-headed. The die was cast and Richard expected to be proud of his bride. "Do we go up to the suite he booked for me?"

"Yes. I...uh...this way to the elevators. I have the key."

Anne Lester was clearly flustered, worrying about having put a foot wrong in what she undoubtedly saw as an extraordinary situation.

"Don't worry about it," Leigh soothed as they set off together. "I know most women would consider Richard a prize. And I do want him." She slid Anne Lester a twinkling look. "But mostly because he wants me."

"Ah!" said the older woman as though a light bulb had gone on in her head. "Well, I've never seen a groom so keen to have everything right for his bride. I do hope you'll approve, Miss Durant."

"The only consideration is that Richard approves," Leigh told her drily. "He's paying the bill."

"Yes. Yes, of course," came the somewhat dazed reply.

The cost of this wedding would mean nothing to Richard, Leigh thought. She wondered if the publicity of it would help his business manoeuvrings in some way. Or was it a strictly personal thing?

Pride...vengeance...satisfaction.

One thing she did know—it wasn't a celebration of love.

And sadness crept into her heart.

No love for Leigh.

But at least Richard needed and wanted her, she fiercely told herself, and that was more than she'd ever had from her family. She would not let them spoil her wedding tomorrow. She would pretend they weren't there. After all, they wouldn't be there...not for her. Only Richard would be there for her.

Only Richard.

CHAPTER EIGHT

His queen...

Leigh stared at the reflection in the full-length mirror, hardly believing the bride she saw was herself. Had Richard envisaged her like this when he chose what she was to wear? She remembered her sisters' wedding dresses—wonderful frothy confections with beaded lace bodices and sleeves and hooped skirts—making them look like fairy-tale princesses. But this...the whole look was incredibly regal.

The dress was medieval in style with a heavily boned damask bodice to mould her curves with amazingly sexy emphasis. A small stand-up collar, trimmed with gold piping, hugged her shoulders and dipped down to highlight the heart-shaped edge of the gold embroidered panel which ran down from her cleavage to a point below her navel. The long sleeves were tightly fitted to her elbows from where they widened to long cuffs embroidered with gold. The fluted crêpe skirt hugged her figure to mid-thigh before falling in graceful folds to allow walking room, and at the back was a sweeping train which also featured a design of gold piping.

Around her neck was a simple gold chain but it suspended a diamond that more than rivalled the size of the diamond in her ring. Diamond earrings glittered on her lobes, and to top it all, a gold tiara, holding a veil that completed the bridal picture, framing her hair and providing a filmy foil for the striking style of her dress.

The front section of her hair had been drawn up and rolled into a high chignon to hold the tiara. The rest of it had been fluffed out to fan across her bare shoulders before tumbling down her back.

Her face glowed as it had never glowed before, a tribute to the beautician who had worked on it, subtly playing up her eyes, putting colour in her cheeks and painting her mouth a brilliant cherry red.

"No pastels for you with your dark hair and olive skin," she'd said. "We go for a dramatic effect."

Drama...yes, that's what this wedding is, Leigh thought, the king getting his queen. She hoped she could carry off the part Richard had ordained for her once she was on stage. It was a very scary prospect, now she was fully dressed for it. She wasn't used to being a star.

"Your bouquet." Anne handed it to her, a glorious arrangement of cream roses with deep gold centres.

"Did Richard choose this, too?" Leigh asked, lifting the bouquet to smell the rich scent of the blooms.

"Yes. I suggested sprays of little orchids but he insisted on roses."

Their first kiss in the rose garden...had he remembered that? Did the roses signify anything, beyond the fact it was a flower that men had been brainwashed into thinking of? It was probably foolish of her to try to find meaning in everything.

"I must say they do set off the dress," Anne remarked appreciatively.

"Yes," Leigh agreed, telling herself that was the only meaning the roses had, completing the image Richard wanted her to have. Although roses were a kind of homage.

The telephone rang. Anne picked up the receiver, listened, said, "Yes," and hung up. She smiled at Leigh. "The car has arrived and it's time we were leaving. Are you ready to go?"

Leigh took a deep breath and looked distractedly around the suite. Everything had been tidied up. It had been like a railway station throughout the day, people coming and going, delivering things, doing her nails, her hair, her face. Visitors had commented on the magnificent view of Sydney Harbour from the big corner windows. It had been wasted on her, but tonight...tonight she would return to this suite as Richard's wife, and maybe she would look at the lights and wish for real romance.

Was she ready?

Her heart cramped.

She stared at her reflection again. Better to be a queen with a king than a lonely cuckoo. And she'd given her word.

"Yes. I'm ready," she said firmly, ignoring the nerves attacking her stomach.

"You look absolutely stunning, Leigh," Anne warmly assured her. "I don't think I've seen a more beautiful swan."

It evoked a wry laugh. "Just goes to show what experts can do. Thanks for all your work and care, Anne."

"It's been a real pleasure." She grinned. "You're a model bride. No tantrums. No arguments. Not even a show of nerves."

"I'll probably start shaking at the church. In fact, we'd better get this show on the road before I start shaking here."

The car was another stretch limousine, but white this time and decorated with white and gold satin ribbons.

Every little detail seen to, Leigh thought, as Anne helped to arrange her on the back seat. It was good to have someone riding with her, taking care of everything with the knowledge and experience of having done it all before, even if it was a paid wedding director. At least she didn't feel hopelessly alone on this last ride as the unwanted Durant daughter.

The driver timed their arrival at the cathedral to precisely four o'clock. Anne insisted Leigh wait in the car until guests who were still arriving or lingering outside were all directed inside to their seats. Apparently there were ushers hired to do this and one of them signalled the all-clear when it was accomplished.

The process of getting out of the car was carefully orchestrated by Anne so that nothing became disarrayed. The walk to the cathedral was slowly paced, although Leigh's heart was galloping. Once inside, Anne positioned her in line with the main aisle and set about arranging the train of the dress and the veil to her satisfaction.

A pipe organ was playing a hymn and a boys' choir was singing but the sound floated past Leigh's ears. There seemed to be a drum roll in her mind and her hands were trembling uncontrollably. She hoped her legs weren't going to get wobbly at the critical moment.

The hymn ended. Anne stood in front of her, assessing her arrangement, nodded her approval, held up her hand in a signal to someone, then gave Leigh one last smile. "Perfect. Hold it there for a few beats of the wedding march then set off nice and slow, right down the centre line of the aisle. Just aim for Richard. Looking at anyone else might make you veer or put you off balance. Okay?"

"Yes," Leigh whispered, her mouth and throat suddenly dry.

She wished she had a father to hold her arm. It was awful, being on her own, no-one to lean on, no-one to guide her, no-one to shield her from mistakes in front of all these people. But her father lived somewhere in Italy and she'd walked alone all her life so she could do it once more, couldn't she?

Aim for Richard, she repeated to herself, hoping it would have the effect of a calming mantra. She desperately needed tunnel vision because she could see pews filled with people in the nave of the church, people who would undoubtedly crane their heads to watch and appraise and wonder about the bride—the Durant daughter who'd dropped out of sight six years ago. Curiosity and envy and probably considerable pique would be aimed at her, but she couldn't let herself think of that.

Aim for Richard...

The beginning of the wedding march seemed to boom from the pipe organ. Anne moved aside, counting beats with her hand. "Go!" she instructed, and Leigh's foot jerked forward. Get the rhythm right, she screamed at herself. Centre line. Richard at the end of the aisle...a long, terribly long aisle. Movement on either side of her. A blur of faces. Mustn't look. Only at Richard. Gaze steady on him...step, pause, step, pause...

Then he smiled at her, and somehow his smile made everything easier. It was like a beacon drawing her on to a place of safety. Richard would look after her. All she had to do was reach him. She smiled back, her head high, shoulders straight, determinedly maintaining a slow regal carriage, wanting him to be proud of his bride.

The chosen one...that's what I am, she thought. Not a cuckoo, not a cast-off, not a reject...*the chosen one*.

The people in the congregation floated past. Only when she neared the end of the aisle was her awareness caught by the two women who flanked the front pews; on the left her mother, dressed in lavender, on the right...was it Richard's mother in pale apple green? She felt both women staring at her, emanating strong emotions, demanding attention that tore at her composure and tripped her heart into a faster beat.

Not now, she fiercely told herself. This was *her* moment, hers and Richard's. Let the mothers of the bastard children who were getting married today witness and acknowledge that. She wouldn't let either of them beat at her consciousness...mothers who'd visited the consequences of their own sins upon the children who'd been born from them.

Then Richard was holding his hand out to her and sanctuary was within her grasp. She was holding the bouquet so tightly, it took her several moments to unfasten her fingers. Placing her hand in his brought a hot jolt of reality.

He'd spoken to her on the telephone last night—checking there were no problems—but she had not been with him since he'd left her with Anne Lester. In the intervening time, their wedding had somehow gathered a level of fantasy, but his physical touch, the warm flesh and blood contact, brought Leigh thumping down to earth.

This was it!

He was taking her hand in marriage.

From this day forth...

And suddenly she couldn't meet his eyes. Her heart

craved love and she knew she wouldn't see it there. This was a stage show. All the props were in place and the play would go forward and reach its inevitable conclusion. It would be a triumph for Richard. It should be for her, too. She mustn't let it feel hollow. He *was* the man for her.

The minister, a tall, grey-haired man, garbed in ornate vestments, stepped forward to perform the ceremony. There was a rippling rustle of movement as the congregation settled down. Around the altar were magnificent arrangements of creamy roses and massive candelabra. Stained-glass windows shed beams of coloured light.

"We are gathered here today..."

Leigh did her best to concentrate on the words, resolutely holding panic at bay. She couldn't quite keep her voice from shaking when she repeated each phrase of the marriage vow. Richard spoke his in a warm mellifluous tone, as though he relished the words.

"...love, honour and cherish..."

Leigh closed her eyes and willed it to come true. Love was not part of their agreement but maybe it could grow, given enough encouragement. They were honouring each other right now, so that was not in question. But cherish... Leigh yearned to be cherished. If Richard could view any child they had as "precious," might that feeling overflow onto her?

She heard the minister asking if anyone knew of a reason why they should not be wed, and Leigh's breath caught in her throat. Would one of her sisters leap up and denounce her as not a true daughter of Lawrence Durant?

No one spoke.

She breathed again, castigating herself for the wild

concern. Of course, Richard would not have risked any blot on this shining hour. One way or another, he would have covered all contingencies. Nothing would stop the hunter.

He slid a gold ring on her finger. She didn't have one for him. Irrelevant anyway. Hunters didn't need to wear rings. They used them to get what they went after and hold it—whatever was necessary for a successful hunt.

"I now pronounce you man and wife."

The pipe organ boomed forth again, filling the cathedral with uplifting sound.

The minister smiled at them. "You may now kiss the bride."

The boys' choir started to sing "Song of Joy."

Richard's arm swept around her waist, gathering her in to him with an arrogant panache that signalled his mood of joyful triumph. *His wife*—a major step towards fulfilling the terms of Lawrence's will achieved, especially sweet since Leigh was *his* choice and would never have been Lawrence Durant's.

Leigh felt a major fluttering of nerves. The deed was done, for better or for worse. She had no idea where it would take her now and the fatalism that had brought her this far suddenly sprouted fronds of fear. Intense waves of vulnerability quaked through her.

"Look at me, Leigh," Richard murmured.

She had to...had to see...

Facing the truth was better than fretting.

She'd given herself into the keeping of this man and she had to know if all her instincts had been right...or wrong!

In almost paralysing dread, she lifted her gaze, expecting to be hit by a searing blaze of victorious possession. Yet it wasn't so. In his eyes was a soft, caressing tenderness, as though she was a waif of the world he'd taken under his wing. And her heart moved, not in shallow flutters, but deeply, gratefully, feeling he meant to take care of her in whatever ways he could.

He bent his head and his lips grazed softly over hers, making them quiver with the sense of caring he imparted. She didn't think of it as gentling a frightened creature so the show could go on as he wished. To her it was a taste of heaven…on her wedding day.

CHAPTER NINE

THE photography session was intense, mixed as it was with a mini press conference. Once Leigh and Richard arrived back at the hotel, the official photographer Anne Lester had hired was promptly joined by a battery of others from newspapers and magazines. Accompanying them were social reporters who shot their questions between poses.

Leigh was amazed and deeply gratified by the answers Richard gave, virtually denying the marriage had anything to do with business, portraying instead a highly romantic bond between them.

"Leigh chose to make a life of her own away from the Durant interests, but I never lost contact with her.

"In my mind, she was always going to be the woman I'd marry. It was only a matter of waiting until she was ready.

"I first met Leigh when she was fifteen. She was special then. She is even more special now."

He said it all so charmingly, so convincingly, smiling at her as though it was absolutely true, Leigh almost believed it herself. She was so touched by everything he projected, her own answers were influenced by his.

"There was never anyone else for me. Only Richard.

"I left home because I felt a need to become my own person. Richard is so strong, I wanted him to respect my choices.

"This is very definitely the happiest day of my life."

And Richard topped that by declaring, "Leigh and I belong together. It's as simple as that."

A love-match.

Leigh was so exhilarated by this *public* story, she didn't feel nervous at all, standing beside Richard at the entrance to the ballroom, greeting the guests and receiving their good wishes as they streamed in. Richard introduced each one to her, and if they had some important business connection to him, he mentioned it in passing. Social acquaintances didn't rate this particular attention. They tended to gush past. Window-dressing to Richard's success, Leigh thought. Only business associates really mattered to him.

Their families lingered behind everyone else. Whether this was prearranged by Richard and Anne Lester, Leigh didn't know. Her happy, relaxed mood lost some of its buoyancy as Richard introduced his mother, who was not accompanied by a husband. She *was* the lady in apple green, her features very similar to her son's, though her eyes were dark brown, not blue.

"Superbly executed, as always, Richard," she commented, a sardonic tilt to her smile.

"Thank you," Richard returned drily. "My wife, Leigh…my mother, Clare Seymour."

No natural chit-chat between them.

"I'm very pleased to meet you, Mrs. Seymour," Leigh rolled out with a welcoming smile.

She was subjected to a weighing look that questioned, far more than it congratulated her on becoming Richard's bride. She could almost feel the unspoken words… *Do you know what you've taken on?* and was tempted to say… *Yes, I do, because I've been there, too,* but she held her tongue, intuitively aware of wounds that had never been healed in this mother-son relationship.

"Richard has walked alone for a long time," came the slightly rueful remark. "I admire your bravery in marrying him."

"Oh, Richard has never been anything but kind to me," Leigh replied with confidence. "That makes it easy to be brave."

"Kind?" She glanced back at Richard as though it was a totally foreign word to be attached to her son. Then she forced a smile at Leigh, murmured, "Good luck, my dear!" and moved on.

It was an unsettling little contretemps, striking home to Leigh that Richard's mother certainly didn't believe in a love-match. But did she know Richard any better than Leigh's mother knew her? Had she ever been concerned about the heart of the cuckoo in her nest?

Leigh brushed the speculation aside as Richard introduced her to his two older brothers and their wives. So he had been the youngest in his family, too, she thought, as she received their good wishes, which also seemed somewhat constrained. Sibling jealousy, she wondered? They were shorter than Richard, barrel-chested, thicker in the neck and brown-eyed. Very much their father's sons, Leigh surmised, wherever he was. They were followed by two teenage girls, Richard's nieces, who artlessly enthused over the wedding and thanked their uncle effusively for inviting them.

It was a nice little moment, quickly eclipsed by the procession of Leigh's sisters. Caroline led them. Nadine took the opportunity of giving Richard a resounding sister-in-law's kiss as Leigh faced her sharper-tongued sister.

"I'm glad you came, Caroline," she offered politely.

"We had to, didn't we?" came the mocking reply.

"No. It was entirely up to you."

It earned a pitying look. "Wake up, Leigh. The master speaks. We jump or pay."

Was she being nasty or actually stating the truth of the situation? There was no time to question. Nadine took her place. "Well, you have managed to do us proud today," she drawled, envy in her eyes. "Quite a touch of class, little sister."

"Thank you, Nadine."

"Amazing!" Vanessa pronounced. "Truly amazing!"

"A swan?" Leigh couldn't resist suggesting.

It floated over Vanessa's head.

Felicity, coolly elegant as always, leaned forward to express wistful doubts. "I do hope you can keep this standard up, Leigh. Richard will expect it."

"I'll try not to let him down," Leigh drily replied.

Finally, the confrontation with her mother. Despite expecting nothing, Leigh felt her heart twist with mangled hope as Alicia Durant paused to gaze with what looked like rueful admiration at her youngest daughter. She shook her head as though bemused by the situation.

"The ultimate twist," she murmured. "You won't believe this, Leigh, but I find it curiously sweet." In a quick, oddly touching gesture, she reached up and gently stroked Leigh's cheek. "You weren't born for nothing, after all."

Leigh found herself too choked up to make any reply. She'd been born to be Lawrence's son. Now she was the wife of Lawrence's substitute son. Was the failure now seen as a success?

Alicia's hand dropped away. Her mouth tilted in a wry

little smile. "*My* child. I wish Lawrence was here to see it. You are a triumph, Leigh. I hope you play it well." There was a tinge of regret in her voice as she added, "Much better than I did."

Approval? After all these years? Leigh felt torn by it, attached as it was to her marriage to Richard. Was it only this that gave her worth in her mother's eyes? Or was there some different feeling behind that suggestion of regret?

Alicia headed off before Leigh could sort through her confusion, before she herself had said a word.

"Are you okay, Leigh?"

She jerked her gaze up to Richard. "Fine! An interesting comparison—your family and mine."

His eyes sharply scanned hers. "A problem for you?"

"Did you force them to come, Richard?"

He shook his head.

"Pressure them?"

He smiled sardonically. "Wild horses wouldn't have kept them away. There was no pressure applied, believe me."

What he said made sense to her so she did believe him, though Caroline's comment still niggled.

A band struck up and a singer gave an emotional rendition of "I've Finally Found Someone" as Richard led Leigh past the tables of seated guests to the centre of the ballroom where part of the dance floor remained clear. He drew her into his arms and danced with her, just the two of them in front of everyone while the beautiful lyric was played through.

"Did *you* choose this song?" she asked him.

He grinned at her. "Of course. I chose everything. But you, first of all, Leigh."

Her heart turned over. He was giving her all the romance she could have wished for, and if he didn't feel it in *his* heart, he was certainly performing wonderfully for her sake. Or was it a matter of pride for him? She couldn't tell and didn't care at this moment. She loved him for making her *his queen*.

The whole reception was superbly orchestrated. They sat at a table with the people Richard obviously most trusted, very close aides in the power structure he'd built within Lawrence's financial empire. They were comfortable with him and their wives were warm and friendly towards Leigh, putting her at ease. They didn't know her but it was certainly the diplomatic move to make with the boss's bride, and she was grateful for the lack of any tensions.

The music played by the band set an uplifting mood, the food served was excellent, French champagne flowed, and the speeches made were flattering and funny. Leigh was lulled into feeling good about everything. She even forgot Caroline's snipe about Richard until she crossed her sister's path on the way to the powder-room.

"Caroline, wait a moment!" she cried impulsively, reaching out to hold her arm.

"The bride commands," came the derisive reply.

"Don't be like that," Leigh pleaded. "I just want to know what you meant by suggesting Richard forced you to be here."

Caroline rolled her eyes. "Come on, Leigh, you know how it works."

"Please...tell me."

"He's the sole executor of the will. He can hold up probate as long as he likes. In the meantime, we dance to his tune," she clipped out impatiently. Hate-filled frustration flashed out at Leigh as she added, "Your tune, too, now, I expect."

"No!" Leigh vehemently denied. "I will never play Lawrence's game."

"Well, good for you!" Her expression slid into flippancy. "Doesn't change anything, though, does it? Richard holds the power and the purse-strings."

"Did he say he would hold up probate on the will?"

Caroline shrugged. "He's Daddy's man. Par for the course."

"No, Caroline. Richard is his own man," Leigh declared with utter conviction. He wouldn't have married her otherwise.

"Tarred with the same brush," her sister mocked.

Was it true? Leigh wanted to deny it. Richard had categorically stated he hadn't pressured anyone into coming. Caroline was assuming he would follow her father's pattern of behaviour, but that wasn't necessarily correct.

"I don't know about probate, but I'll speak to Richard about your inheritance," she said resolutely. "Perhaps he could arrange an advance on it."

"At what price?" Bitter mockery this time.

It instantly struck Leigh how deeply the scars of Lawrence's influence on their lives went, not only for her. It coloured the thinking of all her family. She gently squeezed her older sister's arm. "No price, Caroline, I swear. It's over...what we all went through. You can make your own choices without fear. Start living the life you want to live. There's no-one to stop you, not me, not Richard, not anyone. You're free now."

Her eyes filled with confusion. "I don't understand. Why did you marry Richard?"

"Because I love him."

"Love?"

Caroline stared at her as though there was no way she could grasp that concept, and Leigh herself was surprised that such words had tripped off her tongue. Had the fantasy of their wedding become real to her?

"I would like us to be true sisters, Caroline," she rushed out with urgent intensity. "Not pitted against each other. Could we try that?"

Glazed eyes looked back at her. "You're a fool, Leigh. Richard is a shark. He obviously chose you because you're a pushover, no-one to get in his way."

"That's not true!"

Caroline's focus sharpened into pale blue daggers of scorn. "Blind stupidity! Better learn to play the game or you'll be the loser again." She gave a wild laugh. "Love! My God! What a joke!"

She broke away, chuckling derisively as she headed back into the ballroom. Leigh watched her, suddenly frightened of the caring Richard was drawing from her. Could she trust him with her heart?

She'd married him.

He was her husband but he wasn't her keeper.

She still had choices. She had always had choices. It was only a question of having the will to exercise them. Today she was Richard's bride because she'd chosen to be, and she was going to do her best to make their marriage work right for both of them. It was wrong to let Caroline's cynical view taint what there was between them. Richard had earned her trust, hadn't he?

So far, a fearful little voice in her mind answered.

Give him the benefit of the doubt, her heart urged.

Keep giving it until you know some other truth with absolute certainty.

And it was that thought she took back into the ballroom, that thought she carried up to their hotel suite, that thought she nursed as she faced him alone...on their wedding night.

CHAPTER TEN

DESPITE all her inner reasoning, Leigh felt almost sick with nerves as she preceded Richard into their suite. They were out of the public spotlight now, and she truly didn't know what truth would emerge in private. How much of their wedding had been *real* to the man she had married, how much had been play-acting to his chosen gallery, how much a manipulation of forces she couldn't even begin to guess at?

A few lamps had been left switched on, lending a soft, romantic glow to the room. She spotted a silver ice bucket containing yet another bottle of champagne waiting for them on the table, along with two flute glasses and a silver dish of strawberries. In an attempt to hide her growing tension, she waved to them and lightly remarked, "We haven't finished celebrating?"

"Just about to begin," he answered, his voice a sensual purr of anticipation.

Her heart skittered. She set her bouquet on the table and swung around. His coat and vest were already off, his cravat dangling, and he was flicking the studs on his dress shirt apart. He grinned at her, his eyes twinkling wickedly. "I thought we might need some refreshment from time to time."

The nights are mine.

Their marriage bargain leapt in Leigh's mind and jangled her nerves even further. Which was silly, she frantically reasoned. She wasn't a virgin. He'd done this

with her before. She'd wanted him. Still did. Why should
tonight be different? He hadn't really meant *all* night,
had he? Not all night, every night. What if it *was* different?

"You can let your hair down now, Leigh," he said
teasingly. "In fact, I'll help you. That tiara might be
tricky."

He left his shirt agape and strolled over to her, standing very close as he unfastened the clips in her hair. She
was hopelessly distracted by the scent of his bare skin,
male and musky, seeming to pulse with an animal vitality. Having freed the tiara, he tossed it and the accompanying veil onto the nearby sofa, then started working
the pins out of the topknot it had encircled.

"You carried everything off magnificently," he murmured appreciatively.

She took a deep breath, trying to concentrate her mind
away from the physical sensations he was arousing with
the soft massage of his fingers through her hair. "Were
you worrying I might fail you?" she asked, wanting to
understand what was going through his mind.

"No. Not even Lawrence could crush your spirit. Why
would I worry that anything else might?"

"You did rather throw me in at the deep end," she
said wryly.

"You're a survivor. Like me."

Was she? As he ruffled the coiled tresses into tumbling loose, she stared at the pulse beat at the base of
his throat, feeling as though she was about to be caught
in a rip tide and swept wherever it took her. Then his
hand was under her chin, tilting it up, and she lifted her
lashes, needing to see what he felt. His eyes blazed into

hers, but it was more an intense probe for knowledge than a desire to take and possess.

"Is this the happiest day of your life, Leigh?" he softly asked.

The fear of giving him too much power over her clutched at her heart. "Am I so very special to you?" she retorted, instinctively challenging him back.

"Yes," he answered simply.

"Then my answer is yes, too."

His eyes softened, darkened. "I didn't want you to ever feel you'd lost out on a proper wedding. No more losing out, Leigh. Not for either of us."

She had never once thought of Richard as a loser. His mouth covered hers before she could comment, and he certainly didn't kiss her like a loser. With sheer seductive mastery he cleared her mind of any coherent thought and kept it under siege with a flood of sensation. Leigh was right back in the summer-house, feasting wildly on the passion he ignited, not wanting it to stop, her response begging for more and more, her arms instinctively winding around his neck to hold him to her, keep him locked into the exciting flow of feeling he generated.

She was barely aware of him unfastening the bodice of her wedding dress. Only when he eased his mouth from hers to murmur, "Let me take it off, Leigh," did she realise the tight fit was no longer tight. Her arms slid from his shoulders as he stepped back, drawing off the sleeves. The boned bodice was shaped like a corselette, no need for a bra. As it was lifted away, Leigh was acutely conscious of her breasts being freed and fully naked to Richard's view.

Still dazed by the desire already stirred, she simply

stood there, eyeing him with aching vulnerability as his
gaze fell to her exposed body. She felt her nipples tight-
ening as tension screamed through her again. Did he like
what he saw? A frenzy of uncertainty stormed through
her mind. In the summer-house she'd been semi-
covered, not completely bare, and the heat of the moment had made such worries irrelevant. But now she was
committed to living with him, night after night…

A slight shake of his head…what did that mean? His
lips curved into a soft, sensual smile. He lifted his gaze
to hers and to Leigh's intense relief, his eyes bathed her
in hot admiration. Her stomach unknotted and started
rippling tremulously again. She was still desirable to
him.

"I've been envisaging you like this these past six
weeks," he said huskily. "Lush, womanly breasts…
even more beautiful than I imagined."

Tingling heat raced over her skin and a surge of pleasure rolled through her mind. Richard had been looking
forward to having her as his bride, thinking of how it
would be tonight. This part of their marriage wasn't
business at all. Not one bit. It was very, very personal.

And she was glad he was standing back from her so
she could watch *him* as he stripped off his shirt, revealing a broad, tanned, muscular chest. It was amazingly
hairless for a man with such thick black hair. His skin
gleamed like smooth satin, a tactile invitation that instantly accelerated Leigh's heartbeat.

"You're beautiful, too," she said, her voice a mere
whisper, awed by the magnificent physique of the man
she had married.

He laughed, a joyous ripple of exhilaration. "Take
your skirt off, Leigh. I want to see all of you."

Her hands moved automatically to obey his command, any shyness she might have felt banished by the totally captivating fascination in watching him discard the rest of his clothes. He was so aggressively male; the taut flat stomach, the strength of his thighs, and most of all that part of him which she had already felt inside her but not seen until now. Its rampant arousal told her his desire was very real and intensely physical.

Despite the terribly compelling distraction of seeing him stripped of clothes, Leigh had managed to step out of her skirt and rid her feet of shoes. Her fingers were fumbling with one of the suspenders on her garter belt, its fastening buried in the band of lace around the top of her white stocking, when Richard spoke, drawing her gaze back to his.

"Leave it! You look incredibly erotic, just like that."

"But…" *He was completely naked,* was on the tip of her tongue. Somehow the protest was rendered meaningless by the blaze of raw desire in his eyes.

"I'll take them off," he asserted gruffly, moving in on her, scooping her so hard against him her breasts were crushed to the hot vital wall of his chest, which swelled and eased as he emitted a huge sigh. "You feel even better than you look…everything a woman should be," he said with exultant pleasure, then kissed her again, his mouth invading hers with a hard, driving eroticism that stoked a raging need for every intimate connection possible between them.

The thick roll of his erection pressing against her stomach was in the wrong place. Blindly urging a more appropriate shift, she lifted herself onto tiptoe, rubbing herself provocatively against him and returning the fierce possessiveness of his kissing, uninhibitedly impatient in her wanting.

Richard's hands glided over every curve of her back, seeming to revel in the indentation of her spine, the smallness of her waist, the soft round cheeks of her bottom. Then to her intense satisfaction he cupped them and lifted her, swinging her with him to the bed, lowering her onto it, bending over her, kissing her breasts, feeding excitingly on them as he unfastened her garter belt.

It was a shock when he drew back from her, standing upright at the foot of the bed...until he propped her foot on his thigh and proceeded to unfasten her stocking and roll it off, slowly, stroking an electric sensitivity along the bared flesh of her inner thigh, behind her knee, down her calf to the sole of her foot. He removed her other stocking with the same sexy, mesmerising procedure.

Leigh found herself holding her breath, her whole being focused on his touch. With the garter belt removed, he peeled off the remaining lacy G-string, leaving her as naked as he was and everything inside her quivering with anticipation. He parted her legs, his fingertips skimming up exquisitely tingling skin. Then to her profound astonishment, he leaned over and his head hovered over the intimate apex of her thighs and he was kissing her *there*!

She half reared up from the bed, her hands scrabbling at his hair to get a hold and lift him away, but when her whole body was struck with piercing streams of the sweetest, toe-curling pleasure, she fell utterly limp, gasping incredulously as her entire nervous system seemed to clench and unclench with ecstatic delight. Impossible to imagine such intense waves of sensation. They swamped her, owned her, and kept building. She squirmed, moaned, writhed, lost every shred of control over herself, and then she was tearing at Richard's hair, begging for release because she couldn't bear it any more.

The very next instant, it seemed, he was surging up, over her, an arm hooking under her hips, lifting, poising, and she felt him pushing forward, filling her with a glorious solidity that answered all the wild craving inside her, and tears of gratitude gushed into her eyes.

"Yes," she sobbed. "Yes…"

"Yes," he echoed, soothing her with kisses as her muscles convulsed around him in blissful delight, and there was an exultation in his voice that echoed through Leigh, arousing the same feeling.

"My wife," he murmured.

My husband, her mind sang.

And the primitive swell of mutual possession was swiftly and beautifully reinforced as they moved rhythmically together, revelling in the physical bonding. There were many intense pleasure peaks for Leigh, so many her body seemed to roll from one to another until gradually they merged into a constant sea of ecstasy and it didn't matter at all that Richard stayed in control, giving her this incredible experience.

He was wonderful, so generous in his caring that she enjoy this with him, making her feel she was everything he wanted in a woman—in his wife—and she felt he was drawing out the wanting because it was just as magical to him as it was to Leigh…this deeply sensuous affirmation of their union.

Eventually it occurred to her that she wasn't really doing anything active for him, just deliciously luxuriating in what he was doing with her. Her arms felt heavy but she lifted them so she could graze her fingertips over the smoothly bunched muscles of his shoulders, slide her palms over his nipples in a gently rotating caress, stroke her nails down over his stomach.

The sharp intake of his breath caused her to look up. His eyes were glittery, staring wildly at her, and suddenly his body bucked into a driving force, and her heart leapt with mad elation as she felt the fierce tension sweeping through him.

New strength poured into her legs and she rocked him into a faster rhythm, faster, fiercer, her hands clawing his back in the need to push him to that same exquisite brink of no return he'd taken her to much earlier. A guttural cry broke from his throat as he tipped over it and joined her in sweet release, sharing the sheer blind ecstasy of floating together on waves of fulfilment.

With a deep sigh of contentment he lowered himself, gently covering her body with his, impressing flesh to flesh on each other, his forehead resting lightly on hers. She hugged him to her, loving him, loving all of him. His arms burrowed under her waist, hugging just as possessively as he rolled them both onto their sides. For a long time they simply lay entwined, content with closeness, their bodies humming with a harmony neither felt inclined to break.

Leigh thought how lucky she was, sure in her own mind that not many men would be as exciting and considerate as Richard. She could not have dreamed of a better lover. He was perfect for her. If this was to be the pattern of their nights, she certainly had nothing to complain about.

She felt prompted to acknowledge how good it had

been. "Thank you for making it so incredibly wonderful for me, Richard."

He sighed, his warm breath wavering through her hair. "That was how I meant it to be...for our first time."

Leigh smiled. His concern that everything be right for her—their wedding and this night—made her even happier. "We might not have got to this second time if I hadn't felt right about the first, Richard," she informed him, letting him know she had no regrets about what had happened in the summer-house.

He stirred, moving slightly away so he could smile at her, his eyes gleaming quizzically. "It did count then?"

"Oh, yes. I might not have agreed to your proposition otherwise," Leigh readily confessed. "For all your arguments, and I won't say there wasn't some strong persuasion in them, marrying you still meant sharing a bed with you."

He grinned. "Well, I'm glad you were satisfied."

"And you?" Leigh felt compelled to ask. "Are you satisfied with me, Richard?"

The grin broke into an elated laugh. "*Extremely* satisfied. I now have everything I want within my grasp. Including you, my darling." He sobered and indulgently stroked her nose. "I think champagne is called for at this point."

He gently extricated himself from her, rolled onto his feet and headed towards the table, moving with the lithe easy grace of an athlete in superb condition, confident in his nakedness, confident about everything.

A little niggle intruded on Leigh's pleasure in him. Was she really *his darling*, or was he simply delighted with her for falling in with his master plan...the means to his end? Once again she cautioned herself against getting too starry-eyed with Richard. On the other hand, she wasn't about to sour what they had together with the kind of bitter cynicism Caroline had shown tonight.

"I can't promise you a son, Richard," she reminded him, intently watching for his reaction to that truth.

He smiled as he lifted the bottle of champagne out of the ice bucket and wrapped the serviette around it. Still smiling, he glanced back at her. "It won't matter if we don't have a son, Leigh."

His blithe attitude threw her into confusion. She sat up to scrutinise him better. "Isn't that why you married me...to fulfil Lawrence's will and get control of the company?" she put to him bluntly.

He popped the cork and shot her a look that seemed to dance with secret amusement, but it was so brief she wasn't sure. He proceeded to fill the glasses as he answered her. "Our marriage is what we make of it, Leigh. Don't let anything else concern you. Getting control of the company is my business, and I don't want to talk about business tonight."

Neither did she. Though the thought she had in the limousine yesterday slid back into her mind. Richard left nothing to chance, nothing he was able to control. A convulsive little shiver ran down her spine. He'd controlled their wedding, controlled their wedding night...

Stop it! she fiercely berated herself. Everything was fine, wasn't it? She had no reason to fear anything with him. Richard was not *tarred with the same brush* as Lawrence Durant. He *cared* about her. Why else would he want to please her so much?

Because she'd be easier to control under the persuasion of pleasure, easier to manipulate to *his* will. *A pushover!*

Agitated by these thoughts which she savagely told herself were influenced by Caroline's warped view, Leigh sat up, instinctively hugging her knees for comfort. Why shouldn't she take what Richard said at face value? There was absolutely no reason not to, at this point. And she wanted to.

He replaced the bottle in the ice bucket, picked up the glasses and swung around, his gaze targeting her again. She had a brief impression of intense purpose encompassing her. Then it was diluted by a whimsical smile.

"You look like a teenager, sitting there like that."

"Well, I'm not," she returned lightly.

"No, thank God! I waited a long time for you to grow up."

"You *weren't* waiting for me," she scoffed, though secretly wishing she could believe it.

His eyes teased as he handed her a glass. "You'd be surprised how many times I was tempted by the passion you projected, Leigh, wanting to feel it differently."

"So now you have." She sipped the champagne, trying desperately not to show his banter could be deeply meaningful to her.

"And very addictive it is," he purred, setting his glass down on the bedside table.

Leigh's heart started to gallop as he stretched out beside her, his thigh brushing hers, reawakening a highly electric sexual awareness of him. He lifted the long thick tresses of her hair and ran his fingers through them.

"I want a child, Leigh," he murmured, a low throb of yearning in his voice. "You're not using a contraceptive, are you?"

"No." She'd considered it part of their marriage bargain that she would get pregnant as soon as possible.

"It doesn't have to be a son."

Surely it made it easier for him if it was. Easier on both of them.

"Neither you nor I have ever had a real sense of family," he went on.

Was that where he felt he'd lost out? She certainly had, and the idea of making a family of their own was suddenly very appealing.

"I want a child with you. It would be a child who would never feel rejected, not by its mother, nor its father. A loved child."

His words flowed through her, grabbing her heart...a loved child...a wanted child... "Yes," she whispered, and saw him stir, growing excited by the thought, arousing excitement in her, too.

She leaned over him and placed her glass on the bedside table. She didn't want any more to drink. She wanted...

Richard paused her where she was. "Straddle me, Leigh," he commanded, his eyes promising more pleasure, and Leigh needed no further encouragement.

As she settled herself over him, her heart pumping wildly at the prospect of feeling all she wanted to feel again, he guided her positioning so he could slide into her, slowly, prolonging the sensation of an exquisite journey to the innermost depth of her, and when he was there, he cupped one of her breasts and drew it to his mouth, drawing so strongly on it she felt an arc of almost searing desire linking to her womb.

A child, she thought, tears prickling her eyes. A family of their own...hers and Richard's...and it felt so right...so beautifully right, there was nothing to fear.

Nothing at all. Richard wasn't like Lawrence Durant. He would be a real father and she would be a real mother...and she hoped they were making their child this very night.

CHAPTER ELEVEN

THEY honeymooned on Norfolk Island, an isolated haven of tranquillity in the Pacific Ocean, a beautiful jewel of nature that was so far from glamour and glitz, Leigh was amazed at its being Richard's choice. Yet it was the perfect place to relax; no crowds, no frantic traffic, and glorious scenery—green valleys, towering cliffs and the magnificent Norfolk pines adding their distinction to the landscape.

Richard had rented a holiday cottage, nestled in the woods above Kingston, with glorious views of Creswell Bay and out to sea. It offered them every private convenience and comfort they could wish for, including a spa house.

They weren't *on show* here, much to Leigh's relief, and they could do as they liked, when they liked, with no unwelcome intrusions. It quickly became apparent this was precisely what Richard wanted since they spent most of their time naked, both in bed and out of it.

The days were long, lazy and intensely sensual. Leigh revelled in the intimacy, the almost constant state of sexual arousal where a mere look or touch could set her heart racing. It seemed to her pleasure-drenched mind that everything was as perfect as it could be between a newly married husband and wife. They were very much in tune physically and Richard was always ready to indulge her in whatever she fancied.

Having the convenience of a hired car, they spent the

occasional morning shopping in the one small town that served the island's population, the occasional afternoon stretched out on the pretty beach at Emily Bay, swimming in the crystal blue waters of the lagoon.

Sightseeing was more incidental than planned, but Leigh decided they should take in some of the history of the island. She had no idea—not the slightest premonition—that her interest in it would lead to rupturing the happy bubble of harmony she'd been living in with Richard.

Norfolk Island had once been an infamous penal colony where convicts had been offloaded from ships and left under a cruel authority to live out their lives as they were ordered. It seemed to Leigh a terrible irony that this beautiful place had been used as a prison, but browsing through the museum made it depressingly apparent how effective it was.

"No escape but the sea, poor devils," she murmured, reading the account of one rebel's fate and wondering if drowning had been better than living under such an appalling regime.

"Yes, it tends to put one's own life in better perspective, doesn't it?" Richard commented.

Leigh pondered this very valid point as they moved on to walk down the hill to the ruins of the pentagonal prison where the convicts had been housed. The neat Georgian cottages they'd been forced to build for government officials still stood in Quality Row, and were still lived in by those who provided professional services to the islanders, but there was little left of the prison, more a grim reminder of what had been here.

Six men to a cell, Leigh had read, and the outline of the cells showed how small a space they had provided.

She couldn't imagine how six men could be crammed into them for sleeping. No privacy. No comfort. Tempers frayed by the enforced closeness.

She sighed over the miseries they must have suffered and ruefully remarked, "I guess you couldn't call Lawrence's mansion a prison. Not like this. But it did feel like one, all the years I was growing up."

"You made good your escape from it, Leigh," Richard answered, glancing at her with warm approval.

Her curiosity was suddenly piqued. "What about you, Richard? What was your childhood like?"

He shrugged. "Lonely."

"You have two brothers," she prompted.

"Who weren't any more company to me than your sisters were to you," he retorted sardonically.

Leigh recalled his mother's slightly incredulous response when she'd said Richard was *kind*. It stuck in her mind as she asked, "Were they unkind?"

"Not particularly. Mostly I was ignored."

She heard a curt note creeping into his voice and sensed he didn't want to talk about that period of his life, but Leigh couldn't resist the urge to know more about him. "Why was that so?"

"They were older. No common interests. They went to live with their father after he divorced my mother. They had no time for me. It's just the way it was," he said dismissively, the curt note stronger now.

Leigh could feel herself tensing up because of it, but she persisted, determined on filling in his background, wanting to understand what had driven him to be where he was now. "How old were you when the divorce happened?"

"Seven."

"And you stayed with your mother."

"Not exactly. I was placed in a private prep school."

"A boarder?"

"Yes."

"At seven?"

"Out of sight, out of mind," he recited cynically.

"Why?"

He gave her a chillingly grim smile. "My mother considered I'd ruined her life. She fell pregnant to the man she wanted, except he had no intention of divorcing his wife for her and promptly dumped her when she suggested it. Then the convenient husband she did have divorced her when he found out I wasn't his."

"Was that when you learnt about your real father? When you were seven?"

"Yes."

Leigh was appalled at a child of seven suffering through the kind of scene she'd been so devastated by when she was eighteen. At least she'd been old enough to leave and survive by herself. Richard had been put away.

"Was the prep school like a prison?" she asked quietly.

He paused, staring off into the distance, past the prison ruins to the rocky shore and the sea beyond. Had he longed for escape, Leigh wondered?

"It wasn't too bad," he answered slowly, "for those boys who could excel at sport. And academically. It was a matter of getting to the top of the pecking order." Again the chillingly grim smile. "That kind of achievement was respected by everyone: staff, pupils, and most pupils' parents."

Leigh didn't have to ask if he had excelled. It was

written in his physique and in his current achievement, being at the helm of the Durant financial empire. She imagined he'd been a king at whatever schools he attended. University, too. She understood now the air of self-sufficency, the control he kept, the drive to have complete mastery over everything in his life.

"Why did you ask your mother to our wedding?"

He turned back to her, his eyes hard and glittering. "Because she's my mother, whether she wants to be or not."

A love-hate possession? Strange how neither of them could quite let go of the women who'd given birth to them. Something deep kept insisting there should be a bond, however tenuous it might be.

"Why do you think she came?" Leigh asked, remembering the note of antagonism, even of bitterness in Clare Seymour's comments.

His mouth twisted. "Because she takes a perverse satisfaction in the position I have attained."

Like her own mother.

A gathering sense of oppression weighed on Leigh's heart as they walked on towards the stone arch of the Hangman's Gate, one very stark part of the prison still standing. The haunting sense of blighted lives in this place added to the sense of her own life and Richard's having been blighted by others' ambitions.

At least Richard had risen brilliantly from the rejections that could have stolen his sense of self-worth, yet he'd been scarred, too. His need for family was just as deep as hers. She wondered if she was already pregnant. If not, it wasn't from a lack of giving it every chance.

She slid Richard a quizzical look. Was that in his

mind every time they made love? Did his pleasure in her have determined purpose behind it?

"What now?" he asked, catching her gaze on him.

The question popped out. "How do you plan to get control of the company if we don't have a son?"

"There are ways and means," he answered offhand-edly.

"Tell me one of them," she insisted.

"Just leave it to me, Leigh."

She caught his arm, halting him, her eyes pleading with his. "I don't want to feel guilty about having a daughter. Please, Richard...I want to know."

He frowned. "There is no reason for you to feel guilty. We're married. We'll have a child. That shows intent to fulfil Lawrence's terms and whether it's a son or daughter won't matter. I'm the sole executor of the will."

Leigh frowned. Caroline had thrown the fact Richard was sole executor at her, as though it wielded power that could affect her family. But how? She shook her head. "I don't understand. How can that work for you?"

"It doesn't concern you, Leigh."

She would not be brushed off, not on this point. "I want it explained to me," she demanded stubbornly.

He grimaced in exasperation. The flicker of annoy-ance in his eyes sank behind a hard, ruthless shield. "Very well. Lawrence's will cannot be probated until its terms are fulfilled. Your mother and sisters cannot collect their inheritance until the will is probated. Which means, in the normal course of events, they have to wait...and wait..."

He bit out the word with grim satisfaction, and Leigh

caught the impression of a deep and abiding hostility towards her family that he'd never even hinted at before.

"...until such time as we do have a son," he went on in a tone of almost bitter relish. "Which may be never. And given your mother's experience of having five daughters, they all have a very strong appreciation of *never*."

Leigh struggled to fit his words and attitude into some kind of comprehensible context. "Doesn't that mean *never* for you, as well?"

His mouth curled and there was contempt in his eyes as he answered, "Sooner or later, your sisters will get impatient for their inheritance. I'm inclined to think one or other of them will sell me the proxy votes of the shares they can't touch. As the sole executor of the will, I'm in a position to make them that offer."

Leigh's mind whirled with everything Caroline had said...the implications...the assumptions...

The bride commands...the bride who might or might not have the son whose birth would release all their inheritances.

We dance to his tune... Your tune, too, I expect.

Sole executor...holds the power and the purse-strings. At what price?

"Will you give them a fair deal?" she blurted out with painful urgency, almost panicking at the thought Richard might manipulate the situation meanly. If he really was *tarred with the same brush* as Lawrence Durant, she would not—could not—live with him.

He cocked a surprised eyebrow at her. "Scrupulously fair."

The terrible turmoil eased slightly.

"I wouldn't want to leave room for any legal come-backs," he added drily.

Pragmatic. And holding unassailable control. It was frightening...that relentless streak in him...yet there was really nothing for Leigh to criticize. Lawrence had made the abominable will, not Richard, and the act of marrying *her* had already undermined it, to which she had agreed.

Justice for her, Richard had persuasively argued, but somehow Leigh now suspected Richard had his own, very personal vision of justice in mind...the something dark and dangerous she'd seen flashes of on the day of the funeral. All her self-protective instincts were quivering as she stared at him, because what she saw was *the hunter*, stripped of the guise of caring lover.

He stood straight and tall and very still, but there was a lethal air about him that made her heart quake. Ready to strike whatever had to be struck, she thought, feeling the banked energy in him as though it were an electric force, ready to zap out and neutralize. A deeply in-grained pride was stamped on his face and the blue eyes were laser-sharp, probing hers with almost clinical de-tachment, looking for weaknesses, sensing all was not right with her.

"Why are you concerned about your sisters?" he asked. "Did they ever give you any caring?"

"No," she conceded.

His whole expression hardened. "They stayed in their father's household for what they could get out of him. They're still parasites, hanging on to get more out of him. Let them go, Leigh. As they let you go."

He was right. She knew he was. She just couldn't feel

that ruthless. "Is that how you feel about your brothers?"

He shrugged. "They didn't leech off their father. Both of them have established their own lives. I respect that. Your sisters have done nothing I could respect. Nothing."

"Perhaps your brothers' father didn't crush all sense of self-worth out of them," she argued. "Lawrence liked having slaves to his will, Richard."

"You weren't a slave to his will," he retorted tersely. "Your sisters saw the advantage to themselves in sucking up to him and took that road."

"Maybe they saw that road as the only way to survive."

"The easiest road," he scorned. "They didn't bother trying to get a self-supporting job. They stuck to the fat of the land that Lawrence provided. And any one of them would have married me to ensure the fat continued."

Leigh couldn't deny it, yet in a way she understood the mind-set of her sisters, brainwashed from childhood to barter for *the fat* which was held up to them as the be-all of life. They had *worked* for what they'd got out of Lawrence, and paid for it, too, in the loss of heart and soul that might have made them fight for something different.

"You don't know what it was like for them, all those years before you came on the scene," she pleaded, disturbed by the revelation of his deep contempt and wanting to lessen it. "The difference between me and my sisters was my mother never sided with me. Which left me isolated," she explained. "My sisters were encouraged to pander to their father. It was what they were taught, trained to do. Don't blame them for what that did to them, Richard.''

He looked incredulously at her. "You defend them? When they wouldn't so much as lift a finger for you?"

She wasn't sure why she was fighting their cause, only that Richard's view of them was merciless and she knew—who better?—there were mitigating circumstances for how they had behaved and the choices they'd made.

Her eyes fiercely challenged his reading of their situation as she answered him. ''As lonely as you might have been in your boarding schools, you had autonomy from a very early age to make what you could of your life, without interference, without the kind of mind punishment Lawrence handed out. Don't judge my sisters, Richard. You didn't live their lives.''

"No, I didn't," he conceded with a mocking twist. "Perhaps isolation was better. For both of us."

She stared at him, knowing he was hiding much from her, just as he'd hid his contempt from her sisters with a layer of surface charm. None of them knew what he thought of them. She didn't really know what he thought of her, underneath what he projected to gain his purpose. Sexual attraction was certainly a given. That could not be faked. But what else was real? What was truly lodged in the heart and soul of Richard Seymour?

Then he smiled and the shifting sands of their marriage gained some solid ground, because surely he couldn't fake the warm appreciation he was beaming at her.

"You are an amazing person, Leigh." He stepped forward, lightly grasping her upper arms, and the warmth in his eyes sizzled into desire. "Let's get out of this depressing place. Go back to the cottage. I can think of much more pleasurable things to do.''

His hold on her suddenly evoked his words from their wedding night... *I now have everything I want within my grasp. Including you, my darling.*

Leigh barely controlled a convulsive shiver. She allowed herself to be led by him because there was really nowhere else for her to go, and his hug around her shoulders was comforting as they walked to the car. She didn't want to feel alone...isolated. It was easy to lose herself in the mutuality of the physical pleasure they shared, and she needed that right now, needed it badly.

Much, much later, lying together on the bed in their cottage, Richard propped on his side, his face relaxed in an expression of happy satisfaction, Leigh once again felt hopeful that something good could be forged with their continued intimacy. Her husband was a very complex man, but she hoped to reach past all the guarded layers, given time.

A whimsical smile curved his lips as he gently stroked her stomach. "Do you suppose our child could have been conceived, Leigh?''

"Well, if you're potent and I'm fertile, I don't see how we could have missed," she said drily.

He laughed and leaned over to kiss where his fingers had grazed, then trailed kisses lower and lower, making Leigh catch her breath in anticipation of what he meant to do. But before her mind was mashed by the sweet pleasure that drowned all thought, it formed a fierce prayer...

Please, God, let our baby be a boy!

A son would end Lawrence Durant's hold on all their

lives. Richard would have what he wanted—ultimate control—and her mother and sisters could go free. Then maybe their marriage could begin to encompass all she desperately needed from it.

CHPATER TWELVE

"WELL, quite clearly, it's a boy," the technician declared, manipulating the green dot on the scan screen so that Leigh could see, beyond any doubt, the sexual definition of the baby in her womb.

Relief swept through her like a tidal wave. No more anguishing over having a daughter and how that would affect everything. She could relax now, and look forward to the birth of her baby. Having a son shouldn't mean so much, but there was no escaping the fact it did to her, if not to Richard.

For the past four months, ever since her pregnancy had been confirmed, it had been a struggle, telling herself over and over that their child was to be welcomed and loved, regardless of its sex. She had a great deal more empathy now for her mother who had delivered five daughters, each one of them denying her the mental and emotional release that a son would have brought. There was a lot of truth in the old saying... walk a mile in your brother's shoes before judging him.

Of course, the baby still had to be safely born, but the scan had assured her his development was perfectly on track, everything normal, and she'd had no problems with her own health apart from a slight queasiness and fatigue, natural side-effects of her pregnancy. So long as she took reasonable care, in another four and a half months, the terms of Lawrence's will would be fulfilled, finally ending his tyrannical rule.

A son...hers and Richard's son...and while it would be Lawrence's *legal* grandson, there was no genetic connection whatsoever to the man whom she could only think of as a sadistic egomaniac. She was glad there was not one drop of Lawrence Durant's blood in her child.

"You can get dressed now, Mrs. Seymour," the technician said, switching on a light to assist the process. She smiled at Leigh. "I hope that having a son is good news for you and your husband."

"Yes, it is. Though he wouldn't have minded a daughter," she added fairly.

"Maybe next time," the technician commented indulgently.

Next time! Leigh couldn't look beyond *this time*! One thing she would make certain of...there would be no more babies until she saw what Richard was like as a father. As a husband, he shared every intimacy with her in bed, but the intricate workings of his mind were still a mystery to her.

It was as though he boxed his life in separate compartments and he only gave her entry to those he considered part of their relationship. He was very adept at blocking her out of no-go zones. Sometimes she picked up things about him at the parties they attended, but he always brushed off her questions when they went home, making love to her so distractingly, Leigh was diverted from trying to know him in other ways.

However, he was a concerned father-to-be, very protective of her pregnancy, and it was wonderful she now had absolute confirmation that all was well. As soon as she left the medical clinic, Leigh pulled from her handbag the mobile telephone Richard had insisted she have with her at all times. It was almost noon and the

February summer heat was fierce so she quickly stepped into the shade of one of the trees along the pavement to make the call.

It was only necessary to press one button as Richard had put his office number in the computerized memory in case of emergency. While this was not an emergency, Leigh was eager to share the results of the scan, and she didn't think he'd mind her interrupting his work on this occasion. If it had been a girl, she might have needed time to work through her feelings before telling him, but a boy...she was smiling as the call was answered.

"Mr. Seymour's office. How may I help you?" a woman's voice rattled off.

"This is Leigh Seymour, Richard's wife. I'd like to speak to him."

"Oh!" A short surprised silence, probably caused by the fact Leigh had never called his office before. "He's in a meeting right now, Mrs. Seymour. Just a moment while I put your call through to the boardroom."

"If it's an important meeting..."

"No, no...you have top priority. I do hope there's nothing wrong," she added in somewhat of a fluster. "I'm buzzing him...he's picking up...Mr. Seymour, your wife is on the line."

Richard's voice burst into her ear, curt and concerned. "Leigh, what's the problem?"

Bemused by the fact that Richard had obviously instructed his secretary that any call from her had *top priority*, Leigh was slow to reply, her mind digesting the amazing fact that she and their baby were more important to him than any business.

"Leigh!" Richard called with urgent intensity. "Where are you? What's happened?"

A smile grew from deep inside her. "I'm fine, Richard. So is the baby. I just thought you'd like to know it's a boy. We're going to have a son."

"A son?" He sounded stunned. "How can you be sure?"

"I've just had a scan." A sudden surge of pride put a ring of triumph in her voice as she announced again, "It's definitely a boy."

Silence for several seconds. Then slowly, reprovingly, "A scan was scheduled and you didn't tell me?"

Guilt wormed through her pleasure in the news. She probably shouldn't have kept the scan appointment from him. It was just that she'd felt she'd cope better with the outcome, if she had some time to get used to it before facing Richard with the sex of their child.

"I didn't want to talk about it," she confessed.

He sighed. "I would have liked to be there with you, Leigh."

His disappointment made her even guiltier. It had been wrong, excluding him from the experience of seeing their child for the first time. "I'm sorry, Richard. It would have broken into your day and..." She faltered, thinking she was breaking into his day right now without the slightest compunction. Her decision to be on her own had been a selfish one, not considering his feelings at all. "I have a video of the scan. You can watch it tonight," she rushed out in hopeful appeasement.

"Ah!" Relief and pleasure in the sigh.

"He's perfect. Everything's as it should be," she assured him, anxious to give the information he would have seen for himself if he'd been with her.

"That's great, Leigh! Great!" More warmth in his voice now. "It really shows he's a boy?"

"No question. I've just come out of the clinic. I thought you'd like to know straight away."

"Yes. Thank you."

At least she'd done right about calling him, Leigh reassured herself. "I'll let you get back to your meeting now."

"A boy…" he repeated as though totally bemused by the thought…not excited, not triumphant, simply bemused.

The sex of their child really hadn't mattered to him, Leigh thought. A son did not represent an extension of his ego, as a son would have been to Lawrence Durant. Richard was not *tarred with the same brush*.

Buoyed by the hope of a happy family future, Leigh eagerly said once more, "You'll see him tonight."

"Yes…tonight…"

She could hear the smile in his voice and it put a light zing in her heart as she said, "Bye now," and disconnected the call.

Walking down to the basement car park, Leigh reflected on the two sides of her husband's character. He could be just as tender as he was ruthless, gentle…strong, warm…chillingly cold.

In company, he maintained a charming politeness that was never broken by any circumstance—the perfect guest, the perfect host. His social skills were as streamlined and polished as she imagined his business skills were. Yet Leigh knew his mind was working on two levels, superficially satisfying other people's requirements while sifting everything they said and did for information that might be useful to him.

She had learned this from the comments he occasionally dropped to her once they were alone. Sometimes she hugged these little confidences, telling herself they proved Richard trusted her enough to reveal his inner thoughts. Other times she worried over what he didn't tell her, aware he kept a great deal to himself.

Nevertheless, in other areas, she couldn't quarrel with his generosity, especially where she was concerned. Like her car, she thought, as she reached it. Anything she fancied, he'd told her. Cost no object. She could have been zipping around in a Porsche or a Ferrari, but she couldn't see herself transporting pottery or picking up essential materials in a sports car. She'd stipulated a wagon, and he'd insisted she have the Mercedes-Benz ML320, the best on the market.

She settled herself in the driver's seat, thinking this ultra-safe vehicle was much more practical for transporting a baby with all the baby paraphernalia, too. Smiling at the prospect, she drove out of the car park and headed for home, taking the road which led to Rose Bay where Richard had purchased the house Leigh had instantly fallen in love with.

It was ultra-modern and north-facing, with every room that overlooked the bay featuring a wall of glass which gave unrestricted views and allowed light and sunshine to pour inside. A happy, friendly, welcoming house, Leigh had thought, and still did, completely the opposite in style and atmosphere to the highly formal and formidable Durant mansion. And situated on the other side of Sydney Harbour, too.

The white walls and tiled floor had given her a free rein in choosing whatever colors she liked in the furnishings. Bright cheerful colors, she thought with satisfaction. Nothing muted or neutral. Maybe it was her

Italian heritage coming out but she liked a sense of positive vibrancy in a room.

All in all, the past four months had been highly eventful, with Richard delivering his half of their marriage bargain, and she delivering hers. It seemed so long ago now that he had first shocked her with his proposition, but it had only been August last year. They'd been married in the first week of October and Leigh had to concede she had little to complain about and much to be grateful for.

Richard was a kind and considerate husband. A fantastic lover. She had a glorious home. What had been the conservatory at one end of the house had been remodelled to serve as a studio for her, with a top-of-the-line kiln built in that most potters would die for.

Everything she'd left in storage at Broome had now been installed. An interior decorator had done all the legwork in finding and acquiring the furniture and furnishings Leigh fancied. House staff had been hired to do the cleaning and the cooking and the gardening. Leigh had plenty of free hours to work as she liked, and was currently dabbling with a crystalline effect in the glazing process, hoping to create a new range of pottery.

Richard had given her back a very privileged life, far more privileged than the one she'd led in the Durant mansion because everything was tailored to her needs and desires. Yet still she craved the sense of being loved, unconditionally loved. Material riches didn't fill that need. And the estrangement with her family was unlikely to be ever bridged.

Since she'd been living in Sydney again, she'd seen Felicity and Vanessa at social events, a first night at the opera, the opening of an art show. Apart from saying a polite "Hello!" that was the only contact she'd had with any of her sisters. Not that she sought contact but it never felt right, being so alienated from them.

In acquiring the designer clothes expected of Richard Seymour's wife, she had once run into her mother at a Double Bay boutique and impulsively suggested they have coffee together at one of the nearby coffee-shops. Her mother had agreed, though Leigh soon realized it was more from curiosity than any thought of trying to start a new relationship with her.

"Are you pregnant?" Alicia had asked directly, once they were seated at a table.

"Yes, I am," Leigh had answered, aware that it might be a relief for her family to know a child was on the way, a child that might release their inheritances.

It evoked an ironic smile and the comment, "Richard wastes no time." Then she'd looked askance at Leigh. "You are aware he's every bit as ambitious as Lawrence was."

"Is he?" she'd countered, not prepared to accept such a sweeping statement.

Alicia had sat back and in a detached way, mused, "I wonder if it will eat up your life as it ate up mine."

Their whole conversation—such as it was—had left Leigh with many disturbing trains of thought which she'd tried to banish, adding up all the evidence that Richard was not in the same mould as Lawrence, and her life was not going to run along the same lines as her mother's.

Occupied by these thoughts, Leigh was barely aware of the trip home. Turning automatically into her driveway, she was jolted by the realization she had arrived without any memory of how she'd traveled here.

Berating herself for not paying proper attention, she garaged her car, but her mind was still revolving around her mother's life. Once inside the house, she went straight to her studio where privacy was assured and put through a call to Alicia Durant.

"Leigh?" her mother asked, a perplexed note in her voice, as though she couldn't imagine why her fifth daughter wanted to speak to her.

"It's not going to be the same, Mother," Leigh asserted. "I've just had a scan. The baby I'm carrying is a boy."

Silence. Leigh's satisfaction in announcing this incontrovertible fact was short-lived. It didn't really prove or disprove anything.

"I see," Alicia drawled. "Does it give you pleasure to ram that down my throat?"

Again Leigh was thrown into guilty confusion by the response to her news. "No!" she cried. "I just wanted to…" She faltered, tongue-tied. How to explain the desperate need to be clear of the past? To tread new ground?

"Share your happiness?" her mother supplied mockingly.

"No," Leigh answered on a desolate sigh. "I don't suppose I can ever expect that. Just tell Caroline, would you?" she asked dully. "And my other sisters. My having a son means they'll be able to collect their inheritances soon after the baby is born."

Tears pricked her eyes. She put the telephone receiver down as the prickling turned into a gush, and fumbled her way to a chair, helplessly surrendering to a huge churning of emotion. Accepting the way things were was only sensible. Her mind acknowledged that. Yet sometimes the hurt couldn't be suppressed. She wanted a mother. She wanted a father. She wanted siblings she could turn to. She wanted Richard to love her. Why couldn't she be *right* for somebody?

Eventually the deep wallowing in misery passed. In rocking herself through it, Leigh found herself hugging her stomach and remembered her baby, the tiny live human being she'd seen on the scan screen, all scrunched up in her womb. A new life would start once her baby was born. She *would* have love. Mother love, if nothing else. And she'd make everything wonderful for her child. He'd never feel deprived of what truly mattered.

Having pulled herself together, Leigh went upstairs to the master bedroom suite, gave her tear-stained face a good wash, tied back her hair, changed into a pair of stretch shorts and a loose T-shirt, then headed downstairs again to lose herself in work for a while. Shaping clay was always soothing.

Her stomach, empty and unsettled, told her to eat, regardless of a lack of appetite. The baby had to be considered. She made a detour to the kitchen where their cook and housekeeper, Rene Harper, was putting away a load of food shopping.

"Ready for lunch, dear?" Rene asked, her cheerful disposition and motherliness beaming at Leigh, who had chosen the rather plump, middle-aged woman above other applicants for those very reasons. She had instinctively liked her, and the liking was more important to Leigh than impressive references.

"Don't worry about me, Rene. I'll just grab a sandwich and a glass of juice."

"I bought some nice avocados. They're very nutritional, you know. Good for the baby."

"Okay. I'll have one of those, too."

She told Rene about the scan as she ate, and the housekeeper emanated delight in the news, chatting on about the charms and characteristics of little boy babies. The conversation put Leigh in better spirits, and on her return to the studio, she set about molding clay with positive enthusiasm.

The afternoon wore on. A knock on the studio door jolted Leigh from her concentration on the vase she was shaping. The clay collapsed on the wheel and she turned towards the interruption with considerable vexation. "What is it?" All staff had been told her hours in the studio were sacrosanct.

The door opened and unbelievably, Rene, waving apologetically, ushered in *her mother*! "Mrs. Durant insisted..."

Leigh rose from her stool, her hands still dripping wet clay, and stared in stunned disbelief at the elegant figure of Alicia Durant, pushing past the housekeeper. Once inside the studio, Alicia stopped still, her gaze distracted by the display of pots and vases on shelves and pedestals. When she looked back at Leigh, her eyes looked as stunned as Leigh felt.

"*This* is what you do?" she asked, a thread of awed respect in her voice.

"Yes," Leigh managed to get out, her throat tight, her chest tight, her whole body tensing up. She nodded a dismissal to the housekeeper. "Thanks, Rene."

The door closed.

Alicia stepped slowly over to a pedestal which held a tall vase in shades of blue which were enhanced by the crystalline effect Leigh had been experimenting with. "Your work?" she asked, touching it as though coveting it.

"Yes."

"It's beautiful." She shook her head. "Truly beautiful."

Doubly dazed by such unexpected appreciation, Leigh could only utter a weak, "Thank you."

Alicia proceeded to walk slowly around the room, examining all the pieces, occasionally touching. Leigh had no idea what was going through her mother's mind, why she'd come, what she intended by this unheralded visit. Nervously, she wiped her hands on her work apron, watching and waiting until her mother had completed her tour. When Alicia finally faced her again, it was with a look of weighing a new assessment.

"I don't know you at all, do I?" she said, seemingly more to herself than Leigh.

"You didn't want to." It was the plain, unadulterated truth, spoken with stark simplicity.

"No, I didn't," Alicia acknowledged. "You were a desperate act that didn't work, Leigh. Most of the time I couldn't even bear to look at you. It was a relief when you left. I've been thinking about it all ever since you called about the baby."

"I'm sorry. I didn't mean to crow over you...or distress you." Leigh heaved a sigh and searched to express her own feelings. "The last time we met, you drew parallels. It frightened me." She looked at her mother in anguished appeal. "I need my life to be different."

Alicia nodded. "I'm glad it's a boy for you, Leigh. I really am. You didn't deserve what you got from Lawrence and me. I hope Richard treats you well."

"Thank you."

"As for the conditions of the will, I made sure Lawrence provided well for me, independently of his life or death," she stated sardonically. "Felicity and Vanessa are quite well set up from their marriages. However, your news will be some relief to Caroline and Nadine. I'll let them know."

"Please...Caroline made reference to it at my wedding."

Alicia made a derisive sound. "She would. She hated Lawrence probably more than you did."

Leigh frowned, not having known that. "Why?"

"Because she's bright and smart and thought she should be the one to take over from him. He scorned the idea. A woman stepping into his shoes?"

Unthinkable to a man like him. "Why did you stay with him, Mother?" Leigh asked, wanting to understand Alicia's choice when it couldn't have been a happy marriage for her.

Her mouth tilted with irony. "Oh, he was powerful and exciting and challenging, and any other man would have been less. I just wasn't prepared to let him go." She eyed Leigh with a wry knowingness. "I imagine you feel the same way about Richard."

Did she? Leigh had never put her feelings in those terms, yet her mother's words—*any other man would have been less*—certainly struck true.

"Right to the end I wanted Lawrence," Alicia went on, her eyes glazing slightly, focused inward. "I look back now on all I did to keep him...what was gained and what was lost...and realize how obsessive I was about it. Maybe it was a sickness..."

She paused, expelled a long breath, then looked ruefully at Leigh. "Do we really have choices? Or are they driven onto us by a complex array of forces?"

It was a very thought-provoking question. Leigh remembered Richard's comment about her choosing to leave home, taking nothing more from Lawrence, but there had been no consciously made choice in her escape from the life that had turned into a traumatic nightmare. She'd run because *she had to*, driven away by the unfaceable. Even her choice to marry Richard had been influenced by many emotional forces.

"Why did you come here, Mother?" she asked, curious about this choice. It didn't feel awkward to ask. The frank conversation invited it.

Alicia shrugged. "No doubt you'll think it strange after all these years of indifference, but I suddenly wanted to know you, Leigh." She made a self-mocking little smile. "Rather too late for the mother-daughter act. Impossible, I would think, for either of us to carry that off. But I would like to get to know the person you are."

Leigh stared at her mother, hardly believing her ears. The offer to bridge some of the gap between them was like a rainbow at the end of years of rain. Afraid it might disappear, Leigh rushed to meet her halfway, cautioning herself at the last second not to sound emotional. "I'd like that, too," she said as casually as she could. "Getting to know you, I mean."

"I'm not a very nice person," Alicia warned.

"I'm interested." Leigh offered a whimsical little smile. "You're still my mother."

"Yes. I am that," she drily conceded. "Perhaps we could meet for lunch in a week or two. Go shopping for baby things."

"Why not? Give me a call when you find it convenient."

"A boy." Alicia grimaced and shook her head. "I would have given my eye-teeth for a boy."

Leigh was instantly sympathetic. "I felt that way this morning before I knew."

Alicia's eyes suddenly warmed. "It's good to be able to talk to you like this. Without recriminations."

She didn't want guilt, Leigh thought. Then, who did?

"So, we can take it from here," Alicia said with a sigh of satisfaction. "I'll leave you to your work now."

"I'll see you out," Leigh offered, starting to undo her apron.

"No. I'll find my way." Her mother walked over and lightly touched her arm. "Thanks, Leigh. I'll be in touch."

And Leigh suddenly felt too choked up to reply. It wasn't a loving touch but it was a reaching out to her. There was no lingering, no further words. Her mother walked briskly to the door, opened it, stepped out, and closed it behind her. Yet Leigh was left with the sense of a much more delicate door opening, different from the one she had given up on, but very appealing all the same.

She took off her apron, no longer interested in working. She wandered over to the sliding glass doors that opened to the garden and stepped outside. A new start, she thought, breathing in the fresh, slightly salty air from the bay, enjoying the breeze wafting through her hair. Her hand lifted to her stomach, tenderly feeling the tight little mound that held hers and Richard's son. A new start for all of us, she resolved.

From now on she would be more open with Richard and encourage him to be more open, too. Feelings should be expressed, not hidden where they gathered too many other meanings and fed on doubts and worries. She wanted to know more about his choices, where he was really heading and what was driving him.

The hunter…

Tonight, she promised herself. Tonight she was not going to hold back from seeking the answers she wanted.

CHAPTER THIRTEEN

"FOR the mother of my son," were the words at the top of the note accompanying the flowers. Leigh's heart lifted every time she glanced at the beautiful arrangement of dark red roses. She'd carried it up to their bedroom so she could keep looking at it while she dressed for the celebration dinner Richard had booked a table for. The scent of the perfect blooms seemed to fill the room, adding more intoxication to the thought...red roses for love.

"Home at six-thirty," he'd written, and it was almost that now. She'd been getting ready ever since the flowers had arrived, but hadn't used the time efficiently, her mind excitedly playing through scenarios of how she and Richard would spend tonight. Her fingers fumbled with the tricky catch on the gold chain with the heart locket that set off her dress, then finally got it right.

She'd deliberately chosen the red, rather clingy dress which skimmed her curves but had a loose enough fall over her tummy not to show the slight bulge there too much. It was buttoned through from the V-neckline to the hem, which made her feel sexy, readily accessible to Richard's touch. She'd left her long hair loose, easily touchable, as well.

Having slid her feet into gold sandals, dabbed perfume onto her pulse points, smelled the roses once more, she hurried downstairs to the home entertainment room to ensure the scan video was ready to play. It was going to look amazing on the huge TV screen Richard had chosen.

No sooner had she satisfied herself that all was as it should be, than she heard the powerful engine of Richard's Jaguar, and raced to the front door to greet him, knowing he would leave the car outside, ready to transport them to the restaurant. He reached the door before she did, opening it as she entered the foyer, and she stopped, taking stock of the man she had married, the father of her child.

Would she do anything to keep him?

And the answer was...probably yes.

"Do I pass?" he asked, cocking one eyebrow quizzically even as a confident grin broke across his face.

She laughed. "Oh, I think you'll do."

"Good! And may I say red becomes you."

He closed the door and in two strides, had her swept into his embrace and very securely held. His eyes scanned hers, checking for an unguarded response as he asked, "You're happy it's a boy?"

Her smile was straight from the heart. "Very happy. And thank you for the lovely roses."

"My pleasure," he said warmly, then carried even more warmth to her mouth, kissing her long and deeply, making her feel loved even though he didn't say the words.

Maybe he would later tonight, Leigh thought, her heart dancing with hope and her body zinging with desire as she led him eagerly to the entertainment room to show him the video image of their son. She picked up the remote control from the coffee table and snuggled up to Richard on the sofa before pressing the play button. He curved his arm around her shoulders and lightly squeezed as the first picture of their baby flashed onto the screen.

Leigh reported as well as she could remember what the technician had pointed out to her. Richard looked totally enthralled by what he was seeing, not commenting at all. She pressed the pause button when the scan was directed at the genital area.

"There…you see?"

Richard grinned. "Well, he certainly has the right equipment for a boy." His eyes sparkled pure wickedness at her. "Built like a bull."

She punched him playfully. "That's all you men think of…potency and performance."

"Hmm…" He carried her down on the sofa and plucked at her top button. "I think my potency is proven, but I'll have to admit performance is very much on my mind."

"We're going out to dinner, Richard," she reminded him, not really caring if their departure was postponed.

"And it must be said anticipation heightens the pleasure," he murmured, bending to kiss the valley between her breasts before slowly refastening the button. His eyes simmered with promises of pleasure as he added, "A slow escalation is in order. Champagne, lobster, tropical fruit…"

"Not too much champagne," she warned. "Not good for the baby."

"Just a sip now and then to put tingles on your tongue."

He was doing it again, Leigh suddenly realized, making her so sexually aware of him and herself, other things faded into insignificance. But did it really matter tonight? It was an occasion for celebration. Why not simply enjoy it? She would still be married to him to-morrow and the next day and the next. Plenty of time to infiltrate his defenses and get closer to the man he kept to himself.

Leigh happily nursed that attitude for the next couple of hours. They went to Doyle's at Vaucluse, famous for its seafood. Richard flirted with her the whole time, charmingly, provocatively, seductively, and Leigh basked in his undivided attention, both laughing and almost squirming with delight at his turning their dinner into a very sensual feast.

The lovely French champagne did tingle on her tongue. It tingled all through her. The lobster was tender and superbly flavored, not needing any sauce to enhance it. The tropical fruit accompanying it gave a delicious contrast of tastes.

So engrossed were they in each other, neither of them had given any notice to the other patrons in the restaurant, not those arriving or those already seated. It surprised both of them when Clare Seymour stopped at their table and greeted them with the words, "Well, you two seem to be having a good time together."

"Mother..." Richard frowned, his gaze darting around to spot where she'd come from. "...I presume you're here with someone?"

"A friend's birthday." She waved at a table where three other ladies were seated, watching curiously.

"I hope you're enjoying your evening, Mrs. Seymour," Leigh offered with a smile, uneasy with the tension that passed between mother and son.

Clare Seymour directed a rather thin smile back at her. "You seem to be celebrating something, too."

"Yes," Leigh agreed, and seeing no harm in imparting the news, added, "we found out today that the baby we're expecting is a boy."

The thin smile took on a derisive twist. "So Lawrence gets his grandson." A steely blue gaze turned to Richard. "Quite a coup for you, although no doubt you engineered that, as well."

"I can hardly direct nature, Mother," he said sardonically. "Now if you don't mind..." He nodded towards her table. "...you are interrupting a rather special evening."

His mother ignored the hint. "It must give you a lot of satisfaction to have accomplished what your father didn't...in *his* marriage bed. And it's your very first child."

"That's enough!" Richard commanded, his face losing all trace of relaxed geniality.

"Five daughters," she jeered, then swung her gaze back to Leigh. "No, of course. Only four. Richard couldn't have married you if you'd truly been Lawrence's. He's rather fixated on legality. Marriage to a half-sister would be too questionable."

Leigh froze. Richard couldn't have married her if she'd been his half-sister? Then Richard had to be...Lawrence's son! It was Lawrence Durant who'd been Clare's lover...Richard's father...

"For God's sake! Keep your bile to yourself!" It was a savage hiss of fury from Richard who was up on his feet, his face thunderous.

Unabashed, his mother turned and patted him on his shoulder. "I congratulate you, my dear! Such remarkable efficiency in carrying through your master plan. I hope Lawrence is turning in his grave. Writhing in it, actually. Getting his taste of hell for spurning what I could have given him.''

Richard gripped her arm and forcibly lowered it. ''All through my boyhood years, I paid for your silence, Mother,'' he bit out in a low seething tone. ''I promise you, it will be *you* who pays if you ever break your silence again.''

The threat was so palpable, it instantly sobered Clare Seymour. Richard released her and she headed back to her table of friends with a very stiff spine...the imparter of news that held no joy and brought no joy...leaving devastation in its wake.

The expression *being turned to stone* equated fairly well with what Leigh felt. Her eyes still had the ability to see, but the rest of her had become a leaden weight, totally lifeless.

''Leigh...''

She didn't want to look at him. The moment she looked at him she would start studying his features, finding traces of similarity to his *real* father. Like his eyes. Were they the same color blue as Lawrence Durant's? What about the cut of his chin? Now that she knew...

''Leigh...'' He sat down, leaned his forearms on the table, head thrusting forward, urgent intensity emanating from him.

She folded her hands in her lap and sat very still because bad things were clustering around her, bad, bad things, and maybe they wouldn't hurt too much if she sat still and tried very hard to contain herself, keeping her gaze lowered, focused on her hands so that everything else could be shut out. Even Richard's voice could be shut out if she concentrated hard enough.

She remembered doing this at her father's table when

she was little. Except he wasn't really her father. He was Richard's father. Funny to think she'd been born to be *the son*, and there'd been no need for it. The son was already born. He'd been fathered with the wrong woman, that was all. So silly, really, that Lawrence hadn't been informed of it. Then this wouldn't have happened. No need. No need for any of it.

Though her mother wouldn't have liked it. No. Maybe her mother would have kept trying for a son anyway, still using the Italian gardener. But Richard wouldn't have had to marry the cuckoo in the nest to get his natural inheritance if he'd confronted Lawrence with the truth. Control of everything would have gone directly from father to son. She would have been left completely out of it.

The solitaire diamond sitting on the third finger of her left hand winked up at her. Her engagement ring. Wedding ring beside it. The only Durant daughter he could marry, the only one who wasn't a real daughter. *The bride of his choice.* What a terrible lie that was. She was his only choice to get what he wanted, what he must feel he had every right to.

It was as her mother had said this afternoon…not really a choice at all, more a decision driven by a complex array of forces.

Nothing to do with love.

Or being special.

The *only* means to the end…that's what she was to Richard. And a hunter always took whatever means was available to get what he wanted.

A hand grasped her arm, urging her up onto her feet as the chair she was sitting on was tilted back. "We're going home," a soft gravelly voice said.

Home…where was home? Where the heart is, her mind answered, but her heart was all minced up and Leigh doubted it could be put together again. Nevertheless, her body got steered out of the restaurant, the arm around her waist making sure she moved along with it. The next thing she knew, a car door was being opened in front of her and she was being lifted onto the passenger seat and strapped in.

It didn't really matter where she was taken, Leigh reasoned. The bottom had dropped out of the world she'd thought she had. Once again she just didn't belong to anyone or any place. She was adrift…alone.

No, that wasn't quite right. There was the baby. Lawrence's grandson. She moaned in anguish at the thought of her child bearing any part of Lawrence Durant's genes.

"Are you all right?"

The sharp concern from the man who had done this to her, without conscience or caring, sheared through the defensive cocoon of shock and snapped something inside Leigh, letting forth a blaze of fury that energized her whole body. Her head jerked towards him and words seethed off her tongue.

"No, I'm not all right! I'm all wrong, Richard. And I doubt I'll ever be right again, thanks to you and the way you've used me."

He glanced at her, a quick blast of focused power. "What my mother said is irrelevant to us."

"Irrelevant!" Leigh heard the shrillness of her voice and fiercely brought it down. "Like hell it's irrelevant! Don't take me for a complete fool, you bastard!"

He gave a harsh laugh. "Oh, yes, I'm a bastard. And if I'd ever told Lawrence I was his bastard son, he would have made capital out of it, so if you think the truth would have ever served me well, forget it, Leigh. Start remembering Lawrence as he was! How he was to you...the bastard daughter!''

"I wasn't *his* flesh and blood! You *were*!'' she shot back at him.

"Do you think he wanted a son who could match him? Beat him?'' he retaliated with biting derision. "Lawrence would have taken as much pleasure in keeping me down under his heel as he took in putting you down, Leigh. That was the nature of the man. Only in remaining an outsider could I force him to respect me.''

She hadn't considered this perspective. It rattled her hastily formed conviction that Richard should have revealed himself. She kept her mouth shut while she thought about his view of his position. What he'd said was probably an accurate reading of Lawrence Durant's character. Would Lawrence have wanted a son capable of competing with him, or would his egomania demand the son be lesser than the father? Add on the illegitimacy of the son and Lawrence would have undoubtedly taunted him with his lack of any legal rights to anything.

"He would have seen it as weakness, Leigh, my telling him I was his son,'' Richard stated with ringing certainty. "A son wanting something from his father. A leg up. Concessions. An easy road to the top. He would not have assessed my abilities fairly. As it was I had to constantly challenge him to win every piece of ground I took over from him.''

Yes, she could see that. But... "You didn't have to work for him, Richard,'' she said bitterly. "With your abilities you could have done anything, gone any-where.''

She saw his knuckles whiten around the steering wheel. "He was my father," came the taut reply. "I'd known that since I was seven, Leigh. Lawrence Durant, one of the most powerful, wealthiest men in Australia...my father. Do you think I could forget that? Put it aside? Leave it alone?"

An angry sound grunted from his throat. "All those days when parents came to watch their children perform at school, to take them out, to give them treats...I thought of him. I thought of how his other children—the children by his wife—were getting the attention and privileges of being his *legitimate* children."

His half-sisters! All four of them...Felicity, Vanessa, Caroline, Nadine...his half-sisters, getting *the fat of the land*, while he got nothing.

Leigh suddenly saw it very clearly...Richard's drive to get *everything*...one way or another. She even understood it, but it didn't make anything better for her. To him, she was just one more tool in his armory to attain the end he'd aimed for. A contingency plan to his master plan.

"The course was set a long time ago," he muttered, and she remembered again the dark, dangerous flashes of passion from him, the sense of ruthless purpose that would not be diverted.

"And I'm a victim of it," she said, feeling hopelessly drained of any significance as a person.

"Not a victim," Richard retorted sharply. "A partner."

Sheer outrage at his duplicity tore through her, spitting the words, "A partner usually knows the plan."

"You did know it," he asserted. "I spelled it out to you the day of Lawrence's funeral."

"Ah, but you failed to tell me the critical part, didn't you, Richard? That I was the only one you could marry. Not *your choice*! *The only one* who could do the trick of bypassing Lawrence's will for you."

He thumped the steering wheel in angry frustration. "Don't tell me that didn't appeal to you, Leigh, because it did!"

Her own anger surged. "You haven't got a clue what appealed to me, Richard Seymour. You never bothered to find out. All that ever mattered to you was I serve your purpose."

"That's not true!" he cried vehemently.

"Liar!" Leigh fired at him just as vehemently.

"I have never lied to you. Never!"

"I'd like to hear how you reason that one to yourself," she scoffed. "Put in a little grain of truth and then it's not a lie? Is that how you do it, Richard?"

"I have *not* lied to you," he grated between clenched teeth.

Leigh scorned any reply to such blatant mendacity. She sat in grimly seething silence as Richard drove what little distance remained to be traveled. It gave her a savage satisfaction to know he was not so coolly in control of the situation any more, directing play as *he* wanted it, but the way he had manipulated her kept stinging like a swarm of hornets.

The moment the car was halted in their garage, she was out of it and into the house, getting away from him as fast as she could without running. Pride forbade running. Naturally he followed. The hunter didn't let his prey go unless he was convinced his chances of containing it were lost. Except he'd slipped up, and slipped up beyond any chance of putting damage control in place.

The bride of his choice!

That was the worst lie...making her feel special...more attractive to him than any of her sisters...*his* sisters whom he couldn't marry. No wonder he hadn't *wanted* them.

She headed up the stairs in a fury of rejection of every nice thing Richard had ever said to her. Sweet persuaders for getting his own way and keeping her blind to it. Caroline was right—a pushover! Trapped by her own vulnerability into believing—hoping—Richard could give her what she most wanted.

It was a joke! The blackest joke of all!

She reached the top of the stairs and paused to fling the gauntlet down at her cheating husband who was just starting up them. "I am not sleeping with you tonight. Nor any night to come. Find yourself somewhere else to bed down because I will not be your...your *patsy* wife any more!"

He looked up at her with a grimly set face and kept coming. Leigh stalked off down the corridor, reached their bedroom, opened the door, stepped inside and slammed the door behind her to punctuate her decision. This was *her* house. It was part of their unholy agreement, and she saw no reason she should end up with nothing when she'd provided him with the inheritance he'd coveted. He could find himself another residence to live in!

She kicked off her shoes and stormed over to the dressing-table, wishing she could tear off the gold chain with the heart locket, but knowing she needed the mirror to see how to work the tricky catch. She was literally shaking with rage and found it impossible to concentrate on the task.

Then the door opened and Richard stepped into the room.

"Get out!" she screeched at him.

He ignored her demand. With a calm arrogance that incensed her even further, he closed the door behind him and stood in front of it with the air of an immovable force.

"I said get out!" Leigh raged, and with violent passion she picked up the beautiful arrangement of red roses and hurled them at him. "Take these with you! They're a lie, too!"

But he didn't go. He didn't move at all. He stood there, determination carved on his face, a relentless strength of will emanating from him, reaching out and winding around her, trapping her in its force field.

"I let you go twice, Leigh," he said quietly. "I will not let you go now. Apart from what there is between us, you are carrying my child, and I will not be cheated out of having my son. Nor will I allow him to be cheated out of having his father."

CHAPTER FOURTEEN

THE father of her child...

Somehow the reminder of Richard's paternity and what it meant to him knocked the rage out of Leigh. She just stood there, staring at him, trembling from the turbulent passion expended while between them shimmered the commonality of their childhoods, both of them cheated of a mother's and a father's love.

Her mind was hopelessly torn. Could she really justify shutting Richard out of their lives on the grounds that *her* love would be enough for their child? A son needed a father, and not just in name. A name wasn't enough. Not nearly enough. God knew both Richard and she were painfully aware of that...the lack of any caring support, the emotional deprivation. And he had told her—told her from the beginning—any child of his would be precious to him.

No use telling herself that was a lie. All the evidence pointed to its being the truth; his caring over her pregnancy, his disappointment at not being with her at the scan today, his enthralment in seeing their baby for the first time this evening. She knew intuitively that all the years of Richard's lonely life would have built a deep resolution to do the very best by any child of his, in every way there was.

"I'm sorry you're so distressed by what my mother revealed," he said gently.

Out of her misery shot a question that hadn't been

answered. "Why didn't *she* tell him? You might have had a father taking an interest in you."

He grimaced. "Pride. My mother took the attitude that since he didn't want her, he couldn't have me. It was a silent revenge, but one that I believe has given her considerable satisfaction over the years."

"So why tell me? Why come out with it tonight?"

"He's dead. No risk of any nasty comeback from him." His face tightened and anger burned in his eyes. "Though *I* shall certainly have something to say to her. She had no right…"

The bitter anger in him inflamed her own at his deceit. "No, she didn't have the right. But *you* should have told me, Richard. Been open with me…"

He shook his head. "I didn't want you to know. Ever. It would have affected how you saw me, how you felt about me." He expelled a heavy sigh. "As it's doing now, despite the fact I'm the same man you happily embraced when I came home tonight."

"No. That was the mask you put on for me," she cried in vehement denial of such a stance from him. "The real man is what I know now."

"So what is different, Leigh? A name I don't even bear? A name that haunted my childhood, as it did yours? A name I hate as much as you do?" He started walking towards her. "Don't let it drive us apart. It's a bond we share. It's a…"

"Stop it!" She thrust out her hands in a warning gesture as she backed away. "Don't you come near me, Richard." Her voice shook with the violence of her physical recoil from him. "If you try to touch me I'll fight you tooth and claw."

He halted near the foot of the bed, yet Leigh felt

crowded, panicky. She grabbed onto the sidepost of the head of the bed, not that it provided any defense against the power Richard emitted, but it did lend her some physical support and she needed it. Her legs felt weak, her knees in danger of buckling.

Richard frowned. "Surely you know I wouldn't hurt you, Leigh. Not in any way."

"You have hurt me!" she hurled back at him. "You lied...and I believed you. You must have known I wanted to believe you, and you fed me what I needed to hear..." Tears blurred her eyes. "...what I needed..."

She choked. The hurt went bone-deep, soul-deep. Impossible to even begin to express what he'd done to her with his lies.

"I didn't tell you everything about myself, Leigh, but I never once lied to you," he insisted quietly, using a calm, soothing tone that agitated her even further.

"You deceived me. You know you did, making me think you liked me best." That was the cruelest cut of all and she would bleed forever from it.

"I did like you best," he softly claimed. "There was no deceit whatsoever in saying you were the bride of my choice."

"You couldn't choose my sisters so there was no choice," she snapped, hating him for trying to refute what was so painfully obvious.

"I wouldn't have wanted them even if I could," he persisted. "I wanted you, Leigh. I always wanted you."

"No...no...no," she howled, frustrated by the relentless beat of his replies. "You didn't choose me for *me*! Who I am...what I am as a person...didn't count!"

"Yes, it did. It most certainly did," he said with intense fervor.

It made Leigh scream, "Don't lie to me! I was the only one who could get you where you wanted to be."

"Yes! The only one," he finally agreed, his voice riven with a passion that tore along her nerves. "Because where I wanted to be was *with you*!"

"That's not true! Not true!" she cried, frantically refusing to believe him because it meant too much and she couldn't bear him twisting the truth any more.

"*With you*, Leigh," he repeated, his eyes blazing at her, projecting a furnace of feeling as he went on, "*with you*...and laying all Lawrence Durant stood for at your feet, to have or dismiss as you chose. *With you*...in the role you wanted me to play before it was time to do it...your champion. *With you*...for the rest of our lives. That's where I want to be!"

She stood poleaxed, dumbfounded, her heart quivering in some profound vacuum that made no sense to her, but he was tugging at it. Dazedly she watched him break into pacing the floor, gesticulating at her as he pumped out more of his feelings in a turbulent torrent of words that did more than tug at her heart.

"You *are* the only one for me. The only one there's ever been in any meaningful sense. It was *you* who drew me to Lawrence's Sunday lunches, not him. I felt an instant bond with you, Leigh, for all you were only a young teenager. I came to protect you. I came to block him. I sat there, willing you not to be crushed, to keep holding to your inner sense of yourself, and when you finally left that household, I felt so proud of you, I went around for days, inwardly cheering, 'She's done it! She's broken free! She'll make it on her own now!'"

He paused, a strangely haunted look in his eyes, some inner conflict working through him. His mouth made a resigned grimace. "It was all I could do to stop myself from going after you then."

"Then?" Leigh echoed incredulously, barely able to get the word out, her mind shattered by his outburst, the eerie answering of dreams she'd secretly nursed and never voiced to him. How could he know them? Had she been so transparent?

He was shaking his head. "It would have been wrong to try to connect with you then." His eyes flashed that conviction at her. "You connected me to Lawrence."

Yes, she had. Her father's man. But he wasn't, and had never been Lawrence's man, and what he said about his feeling for her... her memory clicked back to the day of the funeral...a fellow traveler, he'd said. A fellow traveler on a road few people could know or understand...a bond...

"You needed to be away from it all," he went on. "Needed to find your own road to take. And time...time to grow into the person you were capable of being."

Looking back, Leigh realized the truth of what he was saying, yet for him to have thought it all out back then, when she had run away...had he really?

"I hired the private investigator so I wouldn't lose you. It was also the best way of ensuring you came to no harm. Then I set a search in motion for your real father, thinking he might be someone you could go to, someone who might want to acknowledge you as his daughter, but that didn't prove to be the case."

He paused, appealing to her for understanding. "I would have put you in contact with him, Leigh, if I'd thought he'd be of any help to you. But he was in Italy and I couldn't see good consequences for either side. It seemed best to leave it alone until such time as the knowledge of his circumstances wouldn't add to the hurt you were already carrying.''

Her throat was too constricted by a lump of emotion to make any reply. She had been so suspicious of his motives and here they were, laid out so clearly, how could she doubt his empathy with her situation, his wish to help?

He frowned, recollecting himself. ''I didn't expect Lawrence to die. Another year…two at most…I had the moves planned to take control out of his hands.'' His gaze lifted again, targeting her with a depth of yearning that reached right into her soul. ''I would have come for you then. Would have courted you with everything I could offer.''

And would have swept her off her feet, Leigh thought, dizzied by the sheer obsession of the vision that had encompassed her. His words on their wedding day… *In my mind, she was always going to be the woman I'd marry.* Not a lie. Not even a smooth line for reporters to pick up. The truth. The actual truth.

''Lawrence's death frustrated that plan,'' he went on, grimacing at having that eventuality rob him of his controlling hand. Again his eyes pleaded eloquently with hers…not the hunter…a man in need. ''And you came back for the funeral. No longer a teenager. A woman. A woman so beautiful, I literally ached to have you.''

She shook her head, realizing how hopelessly she had misinterpreted almost everything he'd said and done.

''It's true, Leigh. I swear it,'' he declared vehemently, misinterpreting her response. ''Yes, Lawrence's will came into play,'' he conceded. ''I wanted you to have

it all. I wanted to give it to you. But most of all, I wanted
you. I wanted you so badly, I used everything I had at
my command to win you to me that day.''

In the garden, by the ornamental pool, Richard stating
he wanted to marry her, saying... *I don't suppose you'd
believe me if I said I loved you.* She hadn't believed it.
Not for a moment. And these past four months together,
she hadn't let herself believe it, would have doubted it
even if he'd said the words, which he hadn't. Had he
been waiting for her to say them?

''At the time, I didn't care why you agreed to marry
me. You did. And I thought I could bind you to me...''

''With sex?'' Leigh queried, seeing how it must have
seemed to him with her response in the summer-house,
his concentration on that intimate aspect of their marriage. *The nights are mine...*

His cheekbones were suddenly illuminated by red
heat, his eyes momentarily anguished. ''You responded
to me. Every time. I thought it was the only certain way
I had of reaching you, having you. But I did try to court
you, Leigh. With the wedding, the honeymoon...''

His queen...

And roses...cream ones in her bridal bouquet...and
today...she stared down at the broken red roses scattered
across the floor...his pleasure...her torment...

''I thought having a child...our child...'' he went on,
a deep throb of wanting in his voice, calling to her, telling her everything she had craved hearing from him,
feeling from him. ''Please, Leigh...for him if not for
me...don't shut me out.''

As he'd been shut out most of his life.

She dragged her gaze up, tears filling her eyes, spilling

down her cheeks. He was a blur but it didn't matter. He
was there for her, would always be there for her.

"I love you, Richard," she blurted out. "I thought
you didn't love me, that I was...I was nothing again.
I'm sorry. I..."

He had her wrapped in his arms so fast, Leigh forgot
what she was trying to say. She simply sagged into his
warmth and was grateful for his strength because all she
could do was hang onto him and weep onto his broad
shoulder.

He held her tight, as she needed to be held...no letting
go, ever...and there was such wonderful comfort in
it...the sense of finally having found her home...where
she belonged...*with him*...and all the years of loneliness
were over...the pain of the past slipping away...and
what had been forged out of that pain was this...their
togetherness...unbreakable because it meant so
much...so very, very much...to both of them.

Her tears kept flowing, like a dam burst of all the
feelings she'd kept suppressed, the fears, the uncertainties, the hopes and doubts, the need to be strong and
independent, to protect herself. They could be released,
and released they were as Richard held her, rubbing his
cheek tenderly against her hair, murmuring what he'd
kept hidden in his heart.

"My life is nothing without you, Leigh. From the day
I met you, you gave me a reason for being. A good
reason. So many times over the years, I'd think...this is
for Leigh. Then to have the reality of you since we've
been married..."

His chest rose and fell in a sigh that whispered warmly
over her temples. "Don't ever think you're nothing.
You're everything. The light of my life. The joy. The

woman I love. With you I feel...*right*. Like all the missing pieces have come together. The empty spaces have been filled by you. I don't know if you understand what I mean..."

"Yes. Oh, yes," she answered, the words dredged from the same soul-deep needs he fulfilled. And the well of tears was gone, pushed out of existence by a surge of well-being that carried an exhilarating sense of *rightness*.

She lifted her head to look into the eyes of this man she loved and had wanted on so many levels. They were open to her, clear blue windows, revealing all she needed to see and know, no deceit, no manipulation, his desire for her as raw and compelling as her desire for him.

Their mouths met in a mutual rush to taste it, feel it as fully as they could...love unchained, flying free. For all the pleasure they had taken in making love to each other throughout their marriage, none of it matched this coming together...this giving to each other of all there was in them to give.

Long into the night they touched in all the ways there were, expressing their feelings, confiding them, reveling in them, completing an understanding that would spread over the rest of their lives, a solid foundation on which to build whatever kind of future they planned together. All that really counted was that they would share it.

As they lay in contentment, stripped of every barrier there had been between them, and Richard tenderly caressing the shape of the baby inside her, Leigh suddenly remembered one of the terms in Lawrence's will and felt an instant stab of rebellion against it.

"Richard?"

"Mm?"

"Do we have to name our son Lawrence?"

"No. This child is ours. And he's going to be himself." He leaned over and kissed her stomach just as a tiny foot skated under the surface of her tightly stretched skin. Richard grinned at her. "See? He's making his presence felt. An individual in his own right."

She laughed at his fatuous expression. "I thought it was stated in the will…"

"I can get around that," he said with such careless confidence, Leigh didn't bother pursuing the point.

"What names do you like?" she asked, happy to go along with his choice.

He shrugged. "Whatever you like."

"There are lots of names I quite fancy," she said, wanting him to suggest a few.

He gave her a hopeful look. "Then maybe we could have more than one child so you can use them up."

Leigh was happy to consider this now, certain Richard would be a wonderful father. "Mmm…just how big a family do you have in mind, Richard? Thinking of founding a dynasty?"

She'd meant it teasingly, but he instantly frowned. "No. Not that. Never that," he said emphatically, his eyes sharply scanning hers. "Don't mix me up with Lawrence, Leigh. Once I have control of the company, its holdings can be sold off if you'd like us to be free of it. I don't need any child of mine to step into my shoes."

"I know, Richard," she hastily assured him. "I wasn't lining you up with Lawrence." She smiled at him to show there was no shadow of comparison. "If I'm your queen, you're my king, and a king's family line is called a dynasty, isn't it? Except all our children can abdicate and do their own thing. Right?"

"Right," he affirmed, visibly relaxing again. Then he cocked a hopeful eyebrow at her. "*All* our children?"

"Well, I don't think our son should be an only child. That could be lonely for him."

"My thinking exactly." His eyes danced with delight. "A family of our own, Leigh. From beginning to end."

"Yes," she agreed, knowing what he meant. No child of theirs would ever feel unwanted or rejected, not belonging to anyone, not valued for the person he or she was. From the moment they were born they would be welcomed and loved by their parents, and that emotional security would spread over their lives, from beginning to end.

"It starts with us," Leigh murmured.

"We can do it," Richard said confidently, taking her in his arms again, cuddling her close. "We'll do it together, Leigh. A safe circle of love where they can grow into whatever they want to be."

"Is that the end you're aiming for, Richard?"

"With you, my love. With you."

He kissed her and Leigh knew it was true.

Taking wasn't what the hunt had been about.

Giving was the end goal.

CHAPTER FIFTEEN

IT WAS the biggest party she'd ever organized at their home and Leigh was delighted it was going so well. All the guests, both family and friends, appeared to be in high spirits, enjoying themselves. Of course, a christening party was a happy occasion, and their four-month-old son was a natural star. Better still, Lawrence's will had finally been settled, and the future lay open for new directions to be taken.

Leigh suspected the latter contributed to the congenial mood of her sisters, all of whom had accepted their invitations. It was doubtful she'd ever be close to them, but it was good to have their antagonism towards her lifted, letting her feel she was at least accepted by them as a desirable relation to have, even if it was only because she'd done right by them in having a son.

Or maybe they didn't see her as a thorn in their side any more. It was over a year since Lawrence had died. With his insidious influence removed and fading with the lapse of time, perhaps they were beginning to see through their own eyes. Both Felicity and Vanessa had seemed quite sincere in their comments to her.

"Lovely home, Leigh," Felicity had said admiringly. "Quite a striking use of color. Most unusual."

It would be to Felicity who had always stuck to a classical style, but it was nice that she wasn't critical.

"And the view is wonderful," she'd gone on, detailing what she liked.

It was a pleasant little conversation, as was the one with Vanessa.

"Gorgeous baby, Leigh. He's actually making me feel clucky." She'd looked coquettishly at the new man she had in tow. "Do you think you're father material, Jordan?"

"I shall only be used as your sperm bank if you marry me," he'd answered, obviously very keen.

"Oh, dear! He's putting the hard word on me, Leigh. I think he should prove he can be as besotted a father as Richard before I take him on as a husband. How else can I know what kind of father he'd be?"

Having had a father like Lawrence, Leigh could appreciate where Vanessa was coming from, but watching her sister and Jordan sparking off each other, she hoped everything would turn out well for them.

Richard *was* totally besotted with their son. Observing him now, carrying their baby around their guests, showing him off, one would never guess he controlled a financial empire. He was the epitome of a proud father, adoring his child and wanting everyone else to adore him. Which they should because he was adorable, Leigh thought, smiling over her own pride in their beautiful baby boy.

Having checked there were no hitches with the caterers, Leigh was making her way back to Richard's side when Caroline intercepted her.

"Got a moment, Leigh?" she asked, purposeful intent clearly on her mind.

Surprised, Leigh automatically answered, "Yes. What would you like?"

"To talk." An ironic smile took any spiteful edge off her next words. "If you can spare the time away from playing happy family."

Leigh sensed that Caroline was half-expecting a snub. She smiled to put her at ease, feeling no animosity at all towards her blunt-spoken sister, aware now of the life-long frustrations that had been carved into her soul. "I could do with a breath of fresh air," she said invitingly. "Let's go out to the patio."

Caroline relaxed slightly. "Thanks, Leigh. A bit of space would be good."

They strolled outside together, Caroline swiping drinks off a waiter's tray as they went. She handed Leigh an orange juice and kept a glass of champagne for herself. "Healthy stuff for you and fortification for me."

Leigh wondered why Caroline needed fortification but simply thanked her for the forethought of supplying her with the juice. She was off alcohol while breast-feeding the baby. They found an unoccupied garden bench just off the patio and sat down, ostensibly to enjoy a quiet drink together, although Leigh was acutely aware of her sister's tension. Caroline stared out at the view, sipped her drink, and without looking at Leigh, finally blurted out what was on her mind.

"I owe you an apology. I've been a pig to you and I'm sorry. You got it more right than any of us, Leigh, going out on your own. Got it right with Richard, too. All I can say in mitigation of my bitchiness is I've been screwed up for a long time."

Leigh took a deep breath. This was very touchy

ground. Slowly, softly, she said, "I hope it's better for you now, Caroline."

"Oh, I've got myself more sorted out if that's what you mean," came the wry reply. "I'm going to stop reacting to our dear departed father's rejection of my abilities and carve out a career of my own."

"What in?" Leigh asked with interest.

"Law. It's a challenge I can get my teeth into. And it leads to the corridors of power. I like power. I would have married Richard for it, but it's better if I go after it myself. I don't want it through a man."

Her mother was right, Leigh thought. Caroline was more her father's daughter than any of the others.

"You know, we're all better off that Richard chose you," Caroline mused. "It did set us free…like you said at your wedding…free to make our own choices, without fear." At last she turned her head and met Leigh's gaze full on. "Not that Richard would have chosen any of us," she said ruefully. "It was always going to be you, wasn't it?"

"Yes," Leigh acknowledged.

"And it is love. I can see that now. Not just you. Him, too. You've got it made together, haven't you?"

"That's how it feels, Caroline."

She nodded. "It gives me goose bumps watching the two of you. It's so different. So very different. No tension. Everything feel-good."

"I'm glad you don't mind…"

"Mind! I was wondering if you'd mind if I dropped in now and then. Just to remind myself how it can be. Visit with the baby for a bit?" she added hopefully. "I mean…" Her self-mocking smile held an apologetic appeal. "...I might develop a nice side, given half a chance."

"You'll be welcome any time, Caroline," Leigh said warmly, understanding all too well what her sister needed.

Her relief was palpable. "Thanks, Leigh. The baby's a real darling. I love it when he smiles. Makes my heart melt. Did Richard choose his name?"

"No. I did."

"Well, good for you! It's perfect. Alexander... Alexander the Great!"

Leigh laughed. "He doesn't have to be great, Caroline. As long as he's happy with himself. That's what I want for him. Richard does, too."

Caroline relaxed into a grin. "Well, you can count on this aunt to give him stacks and stacks of approval."

"Stacks," Leigh agreed feelingly, and they both laughed over their mutual understanding of that need. Healing laughter, she thought, and hoped it was a step towards a closer bond between them.

"What are you two cackling over?"

They turned to find Nadine making a beeline towards them, coming from the path that wound through the gardens.

"The lack of approval bestowed on us in times past," Caroline drily explained.

Nadine rolled her eyes as she came to a halt in front of them. "Why spoil a beautiful day with that miserable memory?" She half-turned, pointing back down the path. "Did you place those pots in your garden, Leigh?"

"Yes. They're part of a range I made for outdoor decoration."

Nadine's gaze swung back, a curious look of assessment in her eyes. "Mother said you did pottery. I must say you've got a terrific eye for picking the right spot for it."

"Thank you."

"You know, I never thought you were good for anything, Leigh. But you are."

The blunt declaration was so *Nadine*, Leigh didn't find it offensive. "I'm glad to hear it," she said.

"If you want approval, I'll give you lots of approval for your pots and urns and the way you've used them."

"That's very big of you, Nadine."

Caroline tittered.

Nadine frowned at her. "I'm not kidding. Leigh's really good at this. In fact, I'm planning to buy into a trendy gift shop, now that I've got the money. When it's all settled, I'd like to stock some of your stuff, Leigh. Could we do a deal on it?"

"I'm sure we could," Leigh readily agreed. "And I'm sorry I was such a pain to you when we were growing up."

"Well, you were an awful kid, always getting me into trouble. Then turning up and snaffling Richard. It was a bit much. I really fancied him. And damned if I could see what you had to recommend you."

"Call it chemistry," Caroline intervened sardonically.

"Guess so," Nadine agreed on a sigh. "Still working, too. Who'd have thought I'd ever see Richard Seymour a virtual slave to a woman and a baby. Speaking of whom…"

They all turned at the escalating pitch of a baby's cry in full demand. Richard was striding towards them, making reassuring noises at his son who was not in listening mode. Despite the comfort of his father's chest and the patting that accompanied the soft baby chat, Alexander arched himself against his father's hold and screamed his lungs out.

Leigh leapt to her feet to meet them.

"What's wrong?" Caroline asked.

Leigh threw her a grin. "Feed time. When Alexander decides he's hungry, he has a one-track mind."

"Feed time," Richard said, hastily bundling their son into Leigh's arms. "One thing I can't do," he directed ruefully to Caroline and Nadine.

Alexander instantly stopped yelling and started snuffling around Leigh's chest.

"See? He can smell the milk," Richard explained.

Both women broke into laughter and starting teasing Richard about the limitations of fatherhood. He was answering good-humouredly as Leigh headed inside to satisfy Alexander's needs. Rather than go upstairs to the nursery, she turned down the hall to the studio where she'd put in a rocking chair and a change table for day use. Being at the end of the house, it was a quiet and private place, even today with a party in full swing.

Finding her mother there was totally unexpected. "Taking refuge from the party, Mother?"

Alicia smiled. "Not really. Just thought I'd take a look at what you've been doing recently. Feed time?"

"Yes. Rather urgent."

"Mind if I stay?"

"Not at all."

Leigh settled on the rocking chair and quickly arranged herself to Alexander's satisfaction. Once he was blissfully occupied, she turned her attention to her mother who had strolled over to the blue vase, still on the pedestal where it had stood ever since Leigh had created it.

"You haven't sold this," Alicia commented, touching it again as though she coveted it.

"Would you like to have it, Mother?"

"Oh, I'm sure you're keeping it because it's special to you, Leigh. I wouldn't take it..."

"As a thank-you gift for organizing the catering for me."

"Really?" She swung around, a look of sheer delight in her eyes. "You wouldn't mind parting with it?"

"No. I only kept it because it was my first success with that particular kind of glaze. If it gives you pleasure..."

"It's beautiful! I loved it from the first moment I saw it."

"Then it's yours."

"How kind! Thank you, Leigh. I'll treasure it."

Alicia chatted on about the more current pieces on the shelves while Leigh fed Alexander. Over the past year they'd established a comfortable relationship. Alicia readily handed out advice on where to shop and gave many good tips on being a successful hostess. She rarely opened up about her own personal life but showed a keen interest in Leigh's. Sometimes Leigh felt as though her mother was fascinated by a life she hadn't led, yet might have in other circumstances.

Alicia watched indulgently as Leigh changed Alexander's nappy. He was full of smiles again now, waving his little arms and making happy sounds.

"Amazing, all that black hair."

"Well, Richard and I both have black hair," Leigh reminded her.

"Yes. But he looks more like you, Leigh. His eyes are too dark to turn blue. People might talk of him as Lawrence's grandson, but he's really mine, aren't you, darling?" She leaned over and tickled Alexander's tummy and he blew bubbles at her. Alicia laughed. "Oh, it's going to be fun, having a boy in the family. And not one that has to be like Lawrence."

She sighed and smiled whimsically at Leigh. "You know, I would really like to enjoy a child. I wasn't much of a mother, but if you'll let me try being a grandmother…"

"You *are* his grandmother," Leigh assured her, smiling as she lifted Alexander and passed him to her mother. "Here! Waltz him out to Richard."

"And who's a beautiful boy, mm?" Alicia cooed as she did waltz her grandson out of the studio.

Leigh shook her head in bemusement. Time, she thought, had wrought changes in all of them. Looking back, she realized it had been very unrealistic to have expected the cloud of Lawrence's influence to lift from her family the moment he'd passed away. It might not ever completely lift but it was no longer a darkly divisive cloud. There was acceptance now. Even some tentative reaching out. Hope for something better.

Having tidied the change table and checked she was fit to be seen again, Leigh returned to the party in a happy buoyant mood, until she saw her mother, still holding Alexander, *and chatting to Clare Seymour.*

Tension instantly screamed along Leigh's nerves. Was

it all right? Should she break it up? Where was Richard? Her gaze darted around the crowd, trying to spot him, her mind awhirl with awful possibilities.

She didn't really *know* his mother, only that the situation between Clare and Richard had eased. He had gone to talk to her the day after the shocking revelation at Doyle's and Leigh had begged him not to use threats to force a maintenance of silence.

"Be open with her, Richard. Tell her how it's been for you. Tell her how it was for me. Make her see Lawrence wasn't worth wasting her heart on. That he's gone now anyway and there's no reason to hurt us. We didn't do anything to her."

But here Clare was, talking to Alicia, the wife she'd wanted Lawrence to discard...and while a *rapprochement* had been forged between mother and son, might not that old wound to Clare's pride pour forth pus?

Leigh's heart was hammering with fearful uncertainties when her gaze finally picked out Richard. A waiter, holding a tray of glasses head high, had momentarily obscured a view of him, but he actually stood only a couple of meters away from the two women and he was watching them. Leigh's wild pulse rate slowed as she saw that his face was relaxed. There was even a bemused little smile playing over his lips.

It had to be all right, she swiftly reasoned.

Richard would have intervened otherwise.

He must have convinced his mother to let the past go.

Relieved, Leigh hurried across the room, eager to be with the man she trusted to make everything as right as he could, within the parameters of human frailties. Long gone were the doubts about trusting her heart with him.

Richard had proved over and over again how safe that trust was.

Somehow he must have sensed her coming. His gaze swung to fasten on hers before she reached him and his eyes smiled his love for her, filling her with happiness.

His arm was outstretched, ready to gather her close, and Leigh nestled against his side with a sigh of contentment, reveling once more in the sense of belonging with him...Richard, her husband, the partner of her heart, her soul mate.

He dropped a kiss on her forehead and rubbed his cheek on her hair. "Our respective mothers seem to have found a positive interest in common," he murmured.

"Our son is the winner?"

"Our son will always be a winner," he declared warmly.

Leigh rested her head on Richard's shoulder and they both watched Alicia and Clare gazing down at Alexander with indulgent smiles on their faces.

What caused them to look up in unison and both spot Richard and Leigh viewing them together was inexplicable...some sixth sense?...a current of energy tugging at them?...a force of nature being reborn?...a maternal urge awakening?

Suddenly, unexpectedly, touchingly, it seemed there were two mothers, sizing up a son and daughter, and liking what they saw, liking what they represented, liking who they were.

Tears pricked Leigh's eyes, but she didn't cry. She looked up at Richard. His eyes met hers and she saw in them the same sense of something like a miracle...the rejection they'd lived with all their lives finally gone.

"It starts with us," he murmured.

"With love," she answered.

"And giving."

The deepest truth of love...giving. They knew it. And Leigh hoped all their family would. Because love was a gift and it was the one thing that should never, never be wasted or laid waste. It was the most precious thing of all.

*   *   *   *   *

Author's Note

Lawrence Durant is dead from page one of this story, yet as you have seen, he remained a driving force in the lives of everyone in it. Men of great wealth invariably exert power over others.

In the coming months, I invite you to King's Eden— a family empire built from a hundred years of pioneering enterprise, embracing a vast cattle station, mining shares in gold and diamonds, a pearl farm that produces the best pearls in the world, and an air charter business that brings tourism to the great Australian Outback.

This is the world of the legendary King family of the Kimberly, now ruled by Elizabeth, the widow of Lachian, and their three sons—each a King of his own empire.

One by one, these men's hearts will be won by women who dare to challenge who and what the brothers are.

London's streets aren't just paved with gold—they're home to three of the world's most eligible bachelors!

You can meet these gorgeous men, and the women who steal their hearts, in:

NOTTING HILL GROOMS

Look out for these tantalizing romances set in London's exclusive Notting Hill, written by highly acclaimed authors who, between them, have sold more than 35 million books worldwide!

Irresistible Temptation by Sara Craven
Harlequin Presents® #2077
On sale December 1999

Reform of the Playboy by Mary Lyons
Harlequin Presents® #2083
On sale January 2000

The Millionaire Affair by Sophie Weston
Harlequin Presents® #2089
On sale February 2000

Available wherever Harlequin books are sold.

HARLEQUIN®
Makes any time special ™